Christmas Fireside Stories

Diane Allen, Rita Bradshaw,

Margaret Dickinson, Annie Murray,

Pam Weaver, Mary Wood

PAN BOOKS

First published 2014 by Pan Books
an imprint of Pan Macmillan, a division of Macmillan Publishers Limited
Pan Macmillan, 20 New Wharf Road, London N1 9RR
Basingstoke and Oxford
Associated companies throughout the world
www.panmacmillan.com

ISBN 978-1-4472-7683-8

Christmas
Fireside Stories

Contents

CONTENTS

CONTENTS

Christmas Recipes

Christmas at Briar Farm

Diane Allen

It was nearly Christmas at the start of the decade now lovingly called the 'Swinging Sixties', and the Bainbridge family at Briar Farm were rushed off their feet with work to be done before the big day arrived.

'Look Mum, look Dad, it's snowing.' Seven-year-old Carol ran out into the farmyard and looked up to the heavens as large soft snowflakes fell onto her eyelashes and the tip of her upturned nose.

'That's all we bloody well need: twenty-two turkeys to clean, dress and deliver all around the Dales before Christmas Eve, and now it's starting to snow.' Bert Bainbridge swore as he pulled another bunch of tail feathers out of the dead turkey that was to make somebody's Christmas dinner.

'Bert, watch your language, you don't want our Carol coming out with words like that at school.' Agnes

Bainbridge looked up at her daughter, twirling outside in the falling snow next to the barn that had been converted to a slaughterhouse full of oven-ready turkeys for neighbours and friends. 'Remind me next year that I can do without this on the run-up to Christmas. Every year you take on more, Bert, and I've so much to do in the home without plucking and cleaning turkeys.' Agnes felt her stomach lurch for about the twentieth time as she pulled the innards out of a particularly fine specimen. 'By the time I've cleaned, weighed and bagged all these do you think I'll feel like my Christmas dinner?'

'Just hold your noise, our lass, you'll not be complaining when we're getting paid for them. It'll see us into spring. Come back inside here, Carol, you are going to get frozen out there.' Bert stood up straight and leaned backwards, straightening his back by putting his hands on his hips. 'Nobbut another two to go and then we're done. Carol, get hold of this brush and sweep some of these feathers up. Put them in that old animal-feed bag and then our Bob can burn them on a bonfire next time we have one.'

'Dad . . .' Carol moaned; she didn't want to be back in the smelly barn with dead birds bagged up for tomorrow's delivery in the old Austin van.

'Don't you "Dad" me, else Father Christmas won't come. He knows what you've had your eye on in the Co-operative window. He'll struggle getting it down the chimney as it is, without you whining.' Bert winked at Agnes as his next victim was put between his legs to pluck.

'Aye, you've a busy few days; tomorrow we'll deliver these turkeys and then Christmas Eve you can go over and pick your Aunty Brenda up from Cowgill and Uncle Tom from out of Dent. They're stopping with us over Christmas. That is, if I get their beds aired and my baking done.' Agnes knocked a lock of hair out of her eyes with the back of her hand and watched as Carol grasped the brush handle with a sullen face.

'Will our Jim take us over Kingsdale or the boring way round by Ribblehead?' Carol started sweeping up, making more of the fine under-feathers of the turkey fly into the air and causing Bert to sneeze.

'You'll have to ask him, when he's finished the milking; it'll depend on the weather now.' Agnes looked out at the snow-filled sky. It looked threatening: a good covering of snow was all they needed. Two miles out of the nearest village on a rugged Yorkshire fell top, Briar Farm could be quickly snowed in. The small, rough farm track was unpassable for anything other than a tractor with snow chains on its wheels.

'I hope he goes over Kingsdale, I like that road: it's nearly off the edge of the world.' Carol stopped brushing for a minute and thought about the narrow road that led down into the valley of Deepdale and then the journey upward into the small dale of Cowgill. It was there her maiden aunt Brenda lived, while her father's single brother Tom had his home in the village of Dent at the bottom of the dale. It was a Christmas tradition that they came and stopped at the farm for a day or two, and Carol relished each day they stayed. Being the youngest of the family, she was smothered in love and affection from both her aunty and uncle.

'Well, you can go and ask him when you've swept that pile up, and take that Indian headdress that you've made with you – else your father will put it in the rubbish.' Agnes weighed another turkey and wrapped it up in greaseproof paper, wrote the weight on it and the name of the customer who had ordered a turkey. 'And then when we've done we'll put the tree up. Bob got the decorations out of the loft for me this morning.'

'I can put my angel on the top, the one I made at school out of cake doilies. And have we any crackers?' Carol shoved the pile of feathers into the big paper sack that still smelt of cow ration with added vigour. 'And I can make some paper chains before I go to bed and Bob can put them up in the front room.'

'We'll see, our Carol. Now have you swept up, because if so go and get under our Bob's feet instead of ours.' The things to be done before Christmas were weighing heavily on Agnes's mind, and her patience was wearing thin with her youngest child's excitement.

'I'm going, because I've done.' Carol picked up the Indian headdress made out of corrugated cardboard decorated with wax crayon in a striking zigzag pattern, and with the holes filled by an assortment of turkey feathers from the plucked birds. A piece of knicker-elastic held the strip of cardboard together and was just tight enough to fix the stunning headwear firmly on Carol's head. She dropped her brush onto the barn floor and danced her way out of the barn, simulating a Native American war dance, a loose feather from her creation floating down behind her.

Agnes looked around. 'Some sweeping up that is: I could have done better with my eyes shut.'

'Just leave it, Mother, I'll tidy up. We're nearly finished.' Bert pulled the last turkey down from the hook where it had been hanging and started to pluck.

Agnes sighed. If only they were nearly finished; she'd only just begun.

Carol skipped across the farmyard. The snow had stopped and the moon was now beaming down from a cold, frost-filled sky laden with stars. She looked up and whispered, 'Happy birthday, Jesus. Can you make sure we all have a good Christmas and that Father Christmas brings me that big doll from out of the window at Settle.'

She skipped a few more steps and then looked up again and added, 'Sorry, Jesus, I forgot to say thank you.'

'Who do you think you are talking to, loony?' Bob came out of the cowshed carrying a bucketful of milk ready to be passed through cooling equipment in the dairy, and then into milk-kits waiting to be taken by him in the tractor and trailer down to the stand at the end of the farm lane the following morning.

'I'm just wishing Jesus a happy birthday.' Carol followed her older brother back into the cowshed. The smell of the cows and last summer's hay hit her nostrils, making Carol feel warm and at ease in her surroundings. The steady swish of the cows' tails, along with their chewing and the drone of the milking machine, made her feel happy as she watched the big roan cows bat their eyelashes at her.

'You are crackers. There's no such person, and anyway, if he does exist, you are two days early, and he's not going to listen to you anyway.' Bob washed the udder of the next cow to be milked and fitted the milking cups onto its teats, setting the machine into motion to milk the docile cow.

'He does exis . . .' Carol struggled with the word. 'And Mrs Wilson, at Sunday School, says he listens to all good children,' Carol protested.

'Exactly. He's not going to listen to you, you are never good.'

'I am good, our Bob, and he will listen.' Carol nearly started to cry, thinking she was unloved.

'Stop blubbing, I was only teasing. What do you want, anyway, shrimp?' Bob walked between cows and gave the next one to be milked a bucketful of feed.

'Mum says you are going to pick up Aunty Brenda and Uncle Tom and that I can go with you. Which way are we going? Can we go over Kingsdale, I like that way?'

'If it's not snowing.' Bob carried the milk unit and attached it to the next cow.

'And if I make some paper chains tonight before bed will you put them up for me in the front room?' Carol pleaded.

'Yes. Now jigger off and leave me in peace. I'll do whatever you want, just let me get on.'

'Thanks, our Bob, I'll get out of your way now.' Carol hesitated in the cowshed doorway. When she was old enough she was going to marry her big brother Bob, because she loved him.

The next day dawned fresh and frosty. The snow clouds had gone, leaving the surrounding countryside twinkling and sparkling with a slight covering of frosted snow.

The old Austin van was filled to the brim with plucked

turkeys as Carol climbed into the back and sat like a pixie on top of the wheel arch.

'Hold on tight, and don't you fall on any of these birds.' Bert slammed the door shut and twisted the handle.

'You all right back there?' Agnes turned and looked at Carol holding on to the back of her dad's seat while balancing on the wheel arch. 'You'll have more room as soon as we deliver some in Settle, so not far to go before you can kneel on the floor.'

Carol smiled. She was enjoying every moment, because she knew that, as in previous years, with every turkey delivered they'd be invited in, made welcome in people's homes, offered a drink and perhaps, if she was lucky, a small present for her. It didn't matter that there wasn't room for her for a while because that added to the excitement of the day.

The van trundled down the farm track and into the village, making the first drop-off at the village post office.

'I'll not be long here, you two stop in the van. We'll see Harry and his wife over Christmas, so I'll not go in.' Bert carried the designated turkey into the post office and came back smiling, carrying a bottle. 'Here, Mother. Harry and Mary say happy Christmas and they're looking forward to seeing us up at the farm, day after Boxing Day.'

'Aye, that's good of them. I'm looking forward to having them up for a bite to eat. It's not Christmas without friends.'

Carol didn't say anything, but she'd expected a present from Uncle Harry and Aunty Mary, as she was used to calling them, and her Dad had not passed her anything.

'Right, let's knock on: one down, twenty to go!' Bert put the old van into gear and pushed on through the country roads that twisted and twined through the Dales.

Every so often he stopped at outlying farms and houses with his delivery of turkeys and Christmas cheer, while Agnes and Carol dropped off Christmas cards and presents to friends and customers. Every house they called at offered a drink and a catch-up with news and warm Christmas wishes.

'You've done well, our Carol. Look at all the sweets and presents you have in the back of this van. And Father, just you concentrate on driving; I think you've had one too many tipples of whisky. Them little sherry glasses hold more than you think, and Winnie Brunskill's was a heck of a portion.' Agnes held on to her seat as Bert dodged the side of the road.

'Aye, she's a grand woman, is Winnie, always generous.' Bert grinned, his cheeks flushed with drink.

'I'll give you generous, just get us home safe.

It's already dark and getting near Carol's bedtime,' Agnes scolded. She knew he had a soft spot for Winnie Brunskill and her charms.

'Nay, lass, don't get jealous, you know there's only one woman for me. Besides, we're nearly home and it's Christmas, isn't it, our Carol?' Bert shouted back to Carol.

'Yes, Dad.' Carol was kneeling in the back of the van between the two front seats, staring out of the wind-screen at the trees and hedges that looked like weird monsters and creatures from the storybooks she loved to read. Her eyes were heavy with sleep, but it had been a lovely day and, as her mum said, she had been really lucky with presents of tangerines, sweets and wrapped presents that were not to be opened until Christmas Day.

Carol pulled her blankets up around her face. The air in her bedroom was cold and the grey light of morning struggled to brighten up the room through the frosted windowpane. If it hadn't been Christmas Eve, she would have stayed a little longer in bed, not wanting to climb out of her comfortable bunk. But it was no good, she was going to have to face the cold linoleum floor of her bedroom and get dressed before running to the bathroom. She pushed the blankets back and quickly walked across the ice-cold floor to where her clothes for the day were laid out. She pulled off her flannelette pyjamas and pulled on her cabled tights and pants, quickly buttoning her liberty bodice, then adding the woollen jumper her mother had spent hours knitting, before tightening the buckle on her pleated tartan skirt. There, she'd done it. She sat in her bedroom chair and pulled her slippers on, and the image of Sooty adorning them smiled up at her in relief at the warmth from her feet. She walked over to the window and blew hot breath on the frosted-up windows, marvelling at the fern-like pattern made by Jack Frost while rubbing a small hole to look through into the farmyard. She watched as her father carried bales of hay to the cattle in the cowshed, the farm cat following him in the hope of a saucer of milk, and she listened to Bob as he shouted instructions to the farm lad who was employed two days a week. She'd better hurry downstairs: once everything had been fed and the milking done, Bob would want to be off into Dent to pick up their relations.

'Now then, lady, I thought you were going to snooze in bed all day. Our Bob's already been in to see if you've stirred your shanks.' Agnes patted her pastry out on the vinyl-covered kitchen table and rolled it thin with her rolling pin. 'There's a bacon sandwich on the top of the Rayburn: I've kept it warm for you along with a cup of tea. Then you can go and feed the dogs before you set off for Dent. Their dinner's here, in this bucket.' Agnes pointed to a bucketful of scraps and dog food ready prepared for the dogs' dinner and then started to cut out circles of pastry with a biscuit cutter before placing them in bun trays to make mince pies.

Carol helped herself to the sandwich and tea, and in between mouthfuls of bacon and bread helped her mother fill the empty pie cases with mincemeat.

'Not too much, Carol, else it will run out all over my oven.' Agnes supervised until all the cases were full and Carol had finished her sandwich. 'Go on now, them dogs will want their breakfast as much as you. Put your wellingtons on and an extra pair of socks over your tights, and don't forget your coat – it's cold this morning.'

The bucket banged against Carol's legs as she carried it across the yard to the kennels where Spot and Benjie were housed. Both dogs heard and smelt her coming and pulled excitedly on the chains that held them to their kennels. They barked in anticipation of their breakfast and pranced as Carol pulled their dishes out of the kennels and filled both up out of reach of the hungry pair. Once the bowls were full she put them in front of the dogs and watched them eat as if they had never been fed before. The food vanished in a few seconds.

'Are you ready, our lass?' Bob yelled. 'I'm just going to have a cuppa and then we'll be away.'

Carol watched as he brushed his mud-covered wellingtons with the yard brush and then disappeared into the farm kitchen. She ran in after him, leaving the empty bucket outside the kitchen door, and pulled her wellies off in the passageway.

'Which way are we going, Bob? Can I sit in the front?' Carol couldn't control her excitement.

'We'll have to go the bottom way today, shrimp, it's too icy to go over Kingsdale; we'd end up down in Deepdale in a crashed van. You can sit in the front until we pick Aunty Brenda up, and then you and Uncle Tom will have to sit in the back.'

'Ohh!' Carol's face dropped.

'Never mind, I'll go fast over the humps, and then your tummy will feel like jelly.' Bob slurped his tea and picked up the van's keys from the brass keyholder next to the back door.

'You'll do no such thing, you'll take care: those roads are icy,' Agnes chastised as she bent to take her first batch of baking out of the oven.

'Back just about dinnertime, Mum. We'll have a houseful when we're all at home.'

'Aye, and I'm no way near ready. Damn, that hurt!' Agnes put the tray down quickly on the table and licked her arm where she had caught it on the hot oven.

'Are you all right, Mum?' Carol stood in the doorway putting her fur-lined boots on.

'Yes, get gone and then I'll crack on while you are away. Once these are made and this apple pie, I'm winning. You can help decorate the Christmas cake when you return, if you want?'

'Yes, I'll do that, Mum.' Carol skipped out of the door and followed Bob, who had already started the van's engine and was waiting for her.

Carol gazed out of the van's windows at the countryside flashing past. The snowy heights of Whernside, Penyghent and Ingleborough lay like sleeping lions under the blanket of snow, and the magnificent arches of Ribblehead viaduct spread out across the wild moorland of Ribblehead and Batty Moss.

'It's a bit bleak today, our Carol.' Bob smiled at his sister as she peered out of the windscreen. 'Soon be in Dent and then there'll be fun. Aunty Brenda never shuts up, does she?'

'No, and she will insist on kissing me. Uncle Tom's all right though, he tells me stories of when he was in the navy and makes me things.'

The van pulled up outside the whitewashed house that was Aunty Brenda's and both Bob and Carol rushed up the slate steps to the green door with a fox-head knocker, shining in the weak morning sun.

'I heard you pull up, there's no need to knock on the door. Come in, you must be frozen.' Aunty Brenda stood fussing on the doorstep before they could even lift the fox-head knocker. 'Mmm . . . Come here and give your Aunty Brenda a kiss; just look at how much you've grown.' Brenda bent down and kissed Carol, leaving a print of her bright-red lipstick on her cheek. 'And you, Bob, are you courting yet? You are a handsome lad; they must be flocking at your feet.'

Carol wiped the lipstick off her cheek and Bob muttered something about taking her bags as he blushed with embarrassment.

'I bet your mother's running around like a headless chicken.' Brenda picked up her bags and looked around her, checking that the cooker was turned off and the back door locked, and with that she happily locked the front door behind her.

'More like a headless turkey. She's plucked and dressed nearly thirty this year. I don't think my father's in her good books.' Bob put the bags into the back of the van and Carol climbed in along with them.

'I'd be telling him what to do with his turkeys, they'd ruin my nails. Am I in the front? Uncle Tom will have to be a back-seat driver with you, Carol.' Brenda could hardly bend down in her tight pencil skirt as she climbed into the front seat of the van. 'There, let's get going, can't wait to see our Agnes.' Brenda smiled at Bob and urged him onwards.

The next stop was in the cobbled village of Dent. The van rattled over the cobbles, passing the still-running fountain and carrying on to the far end of the village. This time Bob just hooted the van's horn. He knew his Uncle Tom would be ready waiting for him and sure enough he was.

'Are you all right, lad, did you have an easy journey? There's a bit of ice on the road, you'll have to take care.' Tom bent down and puffed on his pipe. 'Now then, Brenda, am I in the back with Carol?' Without waiting for an answer he went around to the back of the van, opened the back door, put his small leather case with washing tackle in and climbed into the back with Carol. 'Now then, Carol, two bits of rubbish together, eh!' Tom laughed and slammed the door behind him, sitting flat on the van's floor, still puffing his pipe.

'Tom, can you put that pipe out, it's filling the van with smoke,' Brenda spluttered.

'Sorry, Brenda, never thought.' Tom damped the pipe with the end of his finger and Carol watched in surprise as his finger seemed to be unscathed by the heat. He put the damped pipe in his pocket and then winked at Carol.

Carol loved her Uncle Tom. He was soft and gentle and always had time for everyone, and he smelt of his favourite smoking tobacco, Kendal Twist. She smiled as he leaned forward and whispered, 'I'm in trouble already.' She giggled quietly.

'I can hear you both. Like peas in a pod, you two are. Bob and me are the sensible ones, aren't we, Bob?' Brenda smiled at her nephew.

'Aye, if you say so.' Bob was just keen to get his relations home as soon as he could and for his mother to take control.

'Come in, come in.' Agnes opened the kitchen door and welcomed her guests with hugs. 'I've got the kettle on and made some sandwiches. There's a leg of lamb in the oven for tonight and a trifle or apple pie in the pantry, so we aren't going to starve.'

'You always feed us too well, Aggie.' Brenda kissed her sister and took her coat off.

'Aye, we never want for owt when we come to Briar. How are you, Agnes? You look well.'

'Thanks, Tom. Aye, we are all well, shattered after Bert and his turkey venture, but, as he says, it keeps a roof over our heads.'

'I don't know how you do it, our Agnes. I said to young Bob, you wouldn't get me with a hand up a turkey's bum.'

'Mmm. Come on into the front room, I'm sure Carol wants to show you the Christmas tree she decorated last night and her paper chains. I'll bring your drinks and sandwiches through.' Agnes had managed to forget that she and Brenda were completely unalike, that Brenda thought herself a lady whereas she just hadn't time to think of painted nails and the latest fashion.

'I'm sure it will be beautiful, pet.' Brenda and Tom followed Agnes and Carol into the welcoming front room, where a fire was blazing and Bing Crosby was crooning 'White Christmas' from the wireless on top of the sideboard.

The Christmas tree stood in the corner of the room with glittering tinsel on its branches and glass baubles reflecting the light from the blazing fire. From corner to corner and pinned up in the centre of the room next to the main light, paper chains made with different-coloured paper festooned the ceiling.

'Carol, it's beautiful, and did you make that angel on the top of the tree?' Brenda squeezed Carol tightly as she beamed at the compliment and nodded her head.

'Aye, it must be Christmas and we are all safe and well and another year's nearly over.' Tom sat in the comfortable chair next to the fire.

'Yes, we've a lot to be thankful for, a bit older and a bit more battered by the world.' Agnes smiled at her guests. 'Now let me get you them sandwiches.'

'Go on up them stairs, Father Christmas won't come if he knows you are down here with us old codgers.' Bert smiled at his daughter as she squashed the last crumb of Christmas cake into her mouth, before bed.

'But Dad, I want to stop up with you and Aunty Brenda and Uncle Tom just a minute longer,' Carol pleaded.

'He's in London already, he'll soon be up here, and if you aren't in bed, he'll not leave you anything.'

'All right, I'm going, but I'm too excited to sleep,' Carol protested.

'Come on, give your old aunt and uncle a kiss and in the morning you'll wake up to find Santa's been.' Brenda held her arms out as Carol kissed everyone goodnight and went reluctantly to bed.

'Tomorrow you can stop up as long as you want, I know you like listening to all of us talking.'

'Really stay up? And have supper with everyone else?'

'If you can stay awake that long. Now come on up them stairs.' Agnes urged her excited daughter up the stairs and quickly put her into her pyjamas and pulled the eiderdown over her, tucking her into bed and telling her to go to sleep quickly.

'Look, it's starting to snow, Father Christmas must be on his way. It's coming down quite heavy so I'm glad we are all safely at home. Looks like it's going to be a white Christmas.' Agnes kissed Carol, smiling as she squeezed her eyes tight shut in the happy knowledge that the following morning there would be presents at the end of her bed. Agnes sneaked out of the bedroom, leaving the door slightly ajar for a chink of light to shine into the darkened room, and Carol was left to dream of the morning.

It was still dark when Carol awoke; she was never awake that early, but this morning was different. In the light from the landing she could just make out the shape of a bulging pillowcase full of things that Father Christmas had brought her at the end of her bed. He'd been! He'd been! He'd not forgotten her! Even though her bedroom was freezing and the outside window ledge was piled high with snow, she leapt out of bed and hauled the pillowcase with its contents onto the bed with her. After putting on the light, she carefully took out each and every present, looking at the labels and feeling each one before unwrapping the colourful paper. There were tangerines and a bag of gold chocolate coins, but most interesting of all, there was a large oblong-shaped present that looked the exact size of the doll she had wanted from the Co-operative. She tore off the paper to meet the blinking eyes of the latest Rosebud doll, the one with dark hair that she had wanted so much. She couldn't believe her luck.

'Well, 'as he been?' Carol's mother and father stood in the doorway, having been woken by the noise from her adjoining bedroom.

'He has, he has! Look at all these things.' Carol ripped open more of her presents. A box of dominoes, snakes and ladders, and right at the bottom of her pillowcase was a present from Aunty Mary and Uncle Harry: two knitted outfits for her new doll.

'How did Aunty Mary know that Father Christmas was going to bring me a doll?' Carol was amazed.

'He probably wrote and told her and said what size it was, seeing you'd been a good girl all year.' Agnes smiled at Bert. A little white lie wouldn't hurt at Christmas.

'He's amazing, is Father Christmas. He knows what I want, where I live and he even talks to my friends and relations, *and* he makes it snow so that he can land his sleigh!' Carol carefully removed her new doll from its box, and gasped in amazement as it said 'Mama' in a small voice.

Agnes and Bert watched their daughter's delighted face.

'Happy Christmas, darling, I'm glad he brought you all you wanted, and your father and I love you dearly.' Tears filled Bert and Agnes's eyes; children made Christmas for them and their baby was growing up too quickly. How many more years would Father Christmas be believed in?

'Happy Christmas, Mum and Dad, I love you too.' Carol jumped out of her bed and hugged them both tightly. She loved them more than a thousand dolls from out of the Co-operative window and always would.

Wishing all my readers a very happy Christmas and a peaceful New Year.

Uncle Percy – A Christmas Memory

DIANE ALLEN

When I was young my Christmases were always made special by a visit from my father's eldest brother, Percy, who arrived on Christmas Eve and stayed with us into the New Year.

My brother Jack would bundle me into the back of our old grey Austin van and we would go and pick up Uncle Percy from the small hamlet of Gawthrop, just outside the village of Dent. This was an adventure in itself as he lived a good twenty miles away from our farm in Austwick, and I loved the long journey alone with my big brother.

Uncle Percy was a veteran of the First World War. He had been left for dead in the trenches of the Somme, until the Germans had found him and taken him prisoner of war. He was a quiet man who still bore the signs of being shell-shocked, and his legs were pitted where shrapnel had entered them. He never spoke of the war to any-one, but you knew he had been through hell. After the war he had travelled the country, odd-jobbing.

I suspect what he saw over in the Somme made him restless and weary of his fellow man and caused him to question what life was all about. Eventually he came back to the dale where he was born to become the local postman. His one love was his garden, where he'd grow dahlias and chrysanthemums, winning medals at all the local shows.

Christmas started with the arrival of Uncle Percy. He'd bring a jar of pickled onions for the Christmas table, a box of Turkish Delight for my mother and a ten-shilling note that was more money than I'd seen all year, for me. In return I'd give him an ounce of Kendal Twist for his pipe and my parents would give him a warm home and a loving Christmas. He'd sit by the fire and talk to my father, and I'd listen in as tales were told of days gone by and relish the fact that I could stay up long past my bedtime because Uncle Percy was staying. During the day he'd teach me the names of great battleships, flowers and plants, and play games of dominoes or draughts with me. For exercise he'd stretch his legs by walking around the garden and farmyard of our sprawling farmhouse up in the fells, his gait awkward from the pain he suffered in his legs. I didn't understand any of the things he'd been through

then; I was young and naive, and all I knew was
that Uncle Percy had come to stay and it wouldn't
be Christmas without him. He was a quiet, gentle
soul who I loved dearly.

Sadly, Uncle Percy died a month before I got
married. If he was alive today, I think he'd smile
when the traditional box of Turkish Delight and
jar of pickled onions are bought at Christmas.
It's the little things that count at this special
time, and the memories of those we love who have
passed on and the love of the ones that are still
with us as we celebrate Christmas together.

Kate's Miracle

Rita Bradshaw

THE NORTH-EAST OF ENGLAND, 1919

'Now you be a good lad and help Ellie look after your little sister, all right, Harry?' Kate Finlay stared into her son's big brown eyes. He nodded solemnly, and she reached out and patted his silky curls, saying in as bright a tone as she could dredge up from the deep despair within, 'I won't be long, hinny.'

Picking up the heavy parcel of washing wrapped securely in brown paper and tied with string, Kate turned to Ellie, her neighbour's twelve-year-old daughter. 'Thanks for watching them, lass. I'll be as quick as I can.'

'That's all right, Mrs Finlay, and take your time, the pavements are treacherous.' Ellie's voice was soft with sympathy. Everyone knew how hard it was for Mrs Finlay since her husband had died nearly a year ago, leaving her with two little ones and no means of support. And her so bonny too, with her golden hair and blue eyes. She'd heard her mam and da talking one night about Mrs Finlay; they hadn't known that she was sitting on the stairs in the dark, earwigging. Her mam had said it was even more of a tragedy than most, Mr Finlay dying, because his parents were the sort who wouldn't give you the drips from their nose, and Mrs Finlay was an orphan. She remembered her da had said something about Mrs Finlay and her bairns ending up in the workhouse, and her mam had gone for him good and proper, calling him Job's comforter. She didn't know what that meant but it wasn't good, if her mam's tone of voice had been anything to go by. Poor Mrs Finlay . . .

Kate squared her shoulders as she opened the back door and the raw north-east wind hit her. It had been snowing for a week, but today, Christmas Eve, there was a break in the relentless storms that had swept the North. Nevertheless, the back alleys, roads and pavements were lethal in places, with snow packed hard on the ground. The grey sky lay low over the town of Sunderland and the wintry gloom predicted more snow before too long. At eleven in the morning it was as murky as twilight and bitterly cold.

She stood for a moment on the snow-covered flagstones in the yard, steeling herself for the walk from Wear Street in the East End, where she rented two rooms in a terraced house, to Park Place West which was a stone's throw from Mowbray Park in Bishopwearmouth. Although only half a mile as the crow flies, the big terraced houses of Park Place West were a world away from the overcrowded, disease-ridden tangle of mean streets that made up much of the East End.

She had to get going, she couldn't stand here all day. Hitching up the carefully wrapped package of washing in her arms – which were already aching – she left the yard and walked along the back lane. She hadn't reached the end of it before her feet were cold and wet from the great holes in the soles of her boots. Even though she'd stuffed the holes with squares of cardboard, her feet were numb before long. But it wasn't physical discomfort that pulled her mouth tight. It was fear. Fear of what was going to happen to Harry and Rebecca; fear of the shadow of the workhouse, which was looming more ominously in the last few days than it had done in the long hard months since Timothy had been gone.

She had tried so hard to keep the three of them together, she thought, slipping and sliding on the icy ground that was like glass in places. She couldn't let it all be for nothing. From the day Timothy had succumbed to the deadly Spanish flu that had swept the country, haemorrhaging blood from his infected lungs and frantically clutching her hands as he had fought to breathe in his death throes, she had worked for anyone and everyone.

Besides caring for Harry, and baby Rebecca, who had only been six months old at the time of her father's death, Kate had taken in washing, gone out cleaning, even tried her hand at paper-hanging and painting ceilings, but the fact that she had to drag two small infants with her had made folk wary about using her services. Eventually, with so many men unemployed now that the war was over, the work had dwindled to just the washing she was able to take in. At the best this brought in only a few shillings a week, and the rent each Friday was half a crown.

She nearly went headlong as her feet slipped from beneath her, and performed a kind of pirouette to stay upright, wrenching her back with enough force to cause her to cry out. Leaning against the wall of a house, she shut her eyes and took some deep breaths, the gnawing in her stomach reminding her that she hadn't eaten for two days. The three of them existed mostly on broth and on the bread she baked with cheap inferior flour, but even so there had only been enough for the bairns over the last forty-eight hours. And in spite of walking miles to the slag heaps at the back of the tram sheds – Harry trudging manfully at her side and Rebecca perched on her back – where she joined the destitute foraging for cinders and fragments of coal, they were weeks behind with the rent.

She hugged the parcel of washing to her, opening her

eyes and straightening away from the wall before making herself continue on. There was no food in the house and barely half a bucket of slack and cinders for the range. She desperately needed the promised two shillings for the washing, and they had certainly been well earned, she thought bitterly. Some of the linen had been badly soiled and had taken hours of soaking and pummelling with the poss stick, and after she had dried everything there had still been the mountain of ironing to tackle.

But it had been worth it. She nodded mentally at the thought. She could buy six penn'orth of scrag ends and vegetables on the way home, and a quarter-stone of flour – seconds, of course – and some yeast to make a batch of stottie cake. It would tide them over the next day or two. After that – she bit hard on her lower lip to quell the panic – after that, she didn't know. The landlord had made it clear he wanted something off the back rent last week and she had nothing to give him. And tonight she would have to take a chance and leave the bairns tucked up in bed once they were asleep and go and rummage for cinders on the slag heap. She couldn't take them with her, not with the weather so bad. If they woke up, then they woke up. She'd be as quick as she could be.

She stopped again to catch her breath; the washing weighed a ton. The streets were devoid of the normal horde of bairns playing their games, but up ahead a group of older boys had made a slide on the icy ground, daring each other to scoot down it at breakneck speed and hooting with laughter when one of them fell. The lad who had ended up on his threadbare backside almost at her feet seemed none the worse for wear, however, scrambling up and grinning at her as he said, 'Happy Christmas, Missus,' before joining his motley bunch of pals.

Happy Christmas. She walked on, passing the boys with a smile and a nod whilst fighting the tears. She hadn't told Harry it was Christmas. What was the point? She had no presents for him, not a thing. Even in the workhouse, brutal as the regime had been, at Christmas each child had received a small stocking made of sacking, holding a bag of sweets, a tangerine and a sugar mouse – courtesy of the Guardians.

She shuddered: not that she could let her precious babies be taken there. For twelve years, until she was old enough to leave school and take the position in service the workhouse authorities had arranged for her, she had suffered the harsh discipline and cruelty of the workhouse system. On the day she had left, it had been with the words of the matron ringing in her ears. 'Now you are leaving us it is my duty to warn you against a weakness I fear may be in your blood,' Matron Shawe had said, her hard eyes sweeping disapprovingly over Kate's golden hair and lovely face. 'You were found by a passer-by when you were just a few days old, still clutched in the arms of your dead mother who was lying huddled in a filthy alley. Clearly, you were conceived in sin and your mother paid the penalty for her wickedness. Do you understand me?'

Trembling, she'd murmured, 'You – you're saying my mother wasn't married when she had me.'

'I'm saying bad blood runs through your veins and you have to guard yourself against it.'

'But – but it may not have been my mother's fault, and—'

The matron had interrupted her icily. 'It is *always* the woman's fault. Your mother was bad. It is natural for men to want what they cannot have and it is up to women to refuse it.'

Kate remembered now how she had looked into the grim, stony face with its hooked nose and little moustache and thought that it was unlikely the matron had had to do much refusing. Nevertheless, she had left the workhouse feeling tainted and ashamed, and for the next couple of years, whilst working as a kitchen maid at High Holmes – a big house on the outskirts of Bishopwearmouth overlooking Barnes Park – she hadn't even dared to glance at a lad. Then, one Sunday afternoon, her half-day off, she and Betsy, the perky housemaid she'd shared an attic room with, had gone for a walk out Tunstall way and met a group of lads. Timothy was one of them and she had liked him; he was nice, but it had been one of his pals, a farmer's son, who had sent her weak at the knees. Matthew Wood hadn't been good-looking, not really: his rough-hewn face was too rugged for that, but he had been big and tall and possessed of a sense of humour that kept everyone laughing all the time. And the very fact that she had been so attracted to him had made her cool and stiff with him in particular, although to be fair she had kept all the lads at a distance. She feared they would see what the matron had seen when they looked at her – that she was tarnished and not like the other lasses.

She and Betsy had walked that way each Sunday afternoon after that but she had left the flirting and carrying-on to her friend. Then, five years ago, just after war was declared as Britons returned from the August bank holiday, Matthew had come to the kitchen door at High Holmes and asked to see her. He was going away to fight, he'd said, but he hadn't wanted to leave without saying goodbye. She had been flustered and painfully shy, and he hadn't said much more. Not with the cook looking out of the kitchen window at them and her hardly daring to raise her head, but he'd asked her to write to him and she had promised she would. And then, just before he had walked away, he had kissed her.

A quick kiss, feather-light, but it had been on the lips. And he had looked into her eyes and smiled his sweet, lopsided smile and she had known then that she loved him and would wait for him forever if he asked her to.

But Matthew hadn't asked her. He'd left, and she had gone indoors and received a stern telling-off from the cook, who'd told her that young men were not allowed to call at the house, war or no war. But she hadn't minded that. Starry-eyed and head over heels in love, she had waited for his letter. A letter which had never come.

It had been Timothy who had told her that Matthew had been killed shortly after the British Expeditionary Force had landed in France. She'd often wondered about that, wondered if Timothy had known how she felt about his friend. And when Timothy had begun to gently court her she had let him, needing the support of his comfort and love. But she hadn't loved him back. Liked him, yes; respected him, but not loved – not in the way that Timothy loved her and she had loved Matthew.

They had got wed eighteen months later, a few days after her sixteenth birthday, and sometime after that, in the autumn of 1916, Timothy had been called up. Before he'd left for France he'd told her, almost casually, that Matthew's parents had received a telegram informing them that their son wasn't dead after all but a prisoner of the Germans. Timothy didn't tell her how long he'd known this, and she didn't ask. It was too late: she was a married woman. She'd also been pregnant with Harry, though she hadn't known this at the time. Timothy had come home once on leave before the end of the war, only for a week, but that was when she had fallen pregnant with Rebecca. It seemed the height of irony that the tough, virile man her husband had been had survived the war, only to contract the Spanish flu within days of returning home and to breathe his last within forty-eight hours.

Matthew had come to Timothy's funeral, along with one or two other friends who had lived through the war which had taken so many young men. It had been the first and last time she had seen him since the soft summer's day he had stood at the kitchen door of High Holmes and kissed her. She'd found herself in turmoil, not least because of the way her heart had leapt when she'd first laid eyes on him standing at the edge of the group of mourners. Hating herself, ashamed and horrified that she could betray Timothy so utterly, she'd taken refuge when he'd expressed his condolences in an icy formality that would have frozen the very fires of Hades. It was only after he had left that another of Timothy's friends had told her Matthew had buried his parents the week before, also victims of influenza. It had completed her disgust at herself.

A snowflake landing on her nose brought her out of

the dark morass of her thoughts. Putting out of her head everything but reaching Park Place West, she quickened her footsteps.

'Well, I'm sorry, Mrs Finlay, but like I said, the master and mistress have taken the bairns to the pantomime and then on to Binns for afternoon tea so I've no idea when they'll be back.'

Kate stared at the housekeeper in despair. 'But she knew I was bringing it today. Can't – can't you pay me?'

The housekeeper drew herself up as though Kate had suggested something scandalous. 'I wouldn't dream of it. You know how the mistress likes to check everything herself.'

Oh yes, she knew all right. Kate choked back hot words. She also knew Mrs Bell was as mean as muck, in spite of her fine house and her husband who was a lawyer. Any laundry would charge double, three times what she got paid, for half the amount of linen. 'I need the money,' she said, as calmly as she could.

'You'll have to come back this evening.' The house-keeper nodded at the parcel. 'Do you want to leave that with me or take it back with you?'

Kate tried one last time. Swallowing the few drops of pride she had left, she looked at the housekeeper imploringly. 'Could you lend me something, Mrs Todd? Sixpence would do, just so I can get the bairns a bite to eat on the way home. I'll pay you straight back this evening once Mrs Bell gives me my money, I promise.'

The housekeeper looked down her thin nose. 'I was raised on the principle of "never a lender or borrower be", and it has served me well. I'm sorry, Mrs Finlay, but you'll have to wait until you see Mrs Bell later on.'

Kate thrust the washing at the housekeeper and turned without another word. She would have to return later, there was nothing else for it.

She kept her back straight as she walked away, but once she was clear of the house her shoulders slumped in defeat. And then her legs flew from beneath her as she slipped on a patch of ice the snow had covered. The pain that shot from her coccyx was so acute she couldn't move for a moment or two, lying on the icy ground as she struggled to remain conscious. Eventually she managed to sit up, waves of nausea causing her to retch although there was nothing in her stomach to come up.

How long she sat there waiting for the pain to subside she didn't know, but she was soaked through by the time she pulled herself up, and shivering uncontrollably.

This was the end. She couldn't carry on. She couldn't.

Misery as deep as the sea swept over her, the hopelessness of her situation too vast for the relief of tears.

But she couldn't let Harry and Rebecca be taken into the workhouse. The thought of them suffering what she had endured was unthinkable. Better they paid a visit to the Wearmouth Bridge and all went together, than that. It would be quick; the water flowed deep and fast, and she could hold them close.

Lifting up her face to the sky, which was full of fat feathery flakes of snow, she said bitterly, 'I thought you are a God who loves the little children? Well, I don't see much evidence of it. It's your Son's birthday tomorrow, isn't it? A time of miracles, when He came to earth as a helpless baby. Then give me a miracle for *my* babies. Or is it true what Reverend Alridge preaches from the pulpit, that the sins of the parents are carried down to the third and fourth generations? Show me you're not like man. Show me you care. *Do* something.'

The thickly falling snow muffled the normal sounds of the streets and it was very quiet, her words seeming to hang in the air.

She brushed the snow from her skirts, her teeth chattering, frozen inside and out. Had she lost her reason? What did she expect, for goodness' sake? A voice coming out of the heavens, saying everything was going to be all right? Divine intervention didn't happen in this cold, hard world, or if it did, God reserved it for people like the missionaries or good upright men of the cloth, not for nobodies like her with bad blood running through their veins.

A sob caught in her throat before she said out loud, 'No. No crying, that will get you nowhere.' And Harry and Rebecca were waiting for her. She had to get home to her babies. The bottom of her back was sore and aching. She walked on.

In spite of the driving snow in her face and the icy wind that cut into any exposed flesh like a razor, Kate was barely aware of her physical discomfort on the trek home, so dark were her thoughts.

On reaching their little back yard, she stood for a moment outside the door bracing herself before opening it and stepping into the kitchen. When she and Timothy had first rented the downstairs of the two-up two-down terraced house after their marriage, she had been thrilled with the two rooms she could call home and grateful that the kitchen held a large range for warmth and cooking. The upstairs folk, an elderly couple, had to make do with a steel shelf over their fire, with a kettle and pots hanging from a bar that they could pull out over the flames.

She had enjoyed making a penny stretch to two and cooking a good meal from cheap cuts of meat, determined to be a frugal housewife. Now the range seemed to mock her feeble attempts to keep them warm and fed.

As Kate entered the house, several things registered at once. Instead of Ellie, it was Ellie's mother, Mrs Kirby, who was sitting at the kitchen table with Harry and Rebecca. There was a bright fire burning in the range instead of the miserable cinders she had stoked up before she left that morning, the smell of pot roast cooking in the oven, and one end of the table was heaped with food. At the other end, where Mrs Kirby and the children sat, the tabletop was strewn with the paper chains the three of them were making.

Kate stood there, unable to speak or move. Mrs Kirby had glanced up as she had entered and now smiled at her. 'There you are, lass. I was just saying to his nibs here that you'd be home soon. Diabolical weather, an' so is that woman, asking for the washing on Christmas Eve of all days. But that type don't consider no one but themselves, do they? How did you get on, hinny? I don't suppose that old trout gave you a bit extra, it being Christmas an' all? Too much to hope for?'

Numbly, Kate murmured, 'She wasn't in – although she knew I was coming, and she hadn't left the money for me. The housekeeper said I've got to go back tonight.'

Mrs Kirby gave one of her expressive sniffs, for which she was well known. 'I hope the lady of the house gets the silver sixpence in her Christmas pudding and chokes on it.'

'Mrs Kirby, what's all this?' Kate was still staring in bewilderment. 'I mean, how . . . who . . .'

'Me an' a few of the neighbours got together and thought you might need a bit of cheering up, lass, that's all. There's a sack of coal over there from Mr and Mrs Hutton.' She pointed to a bulging sack in the corner of the room. 'He gets it cheap, bein' a miner. And we all put together for a few bits an' pieces for the table. My Mick's bringing you a nice turkey tonight when he collects ours from the butcher's, an'—' Mrs Kirby lowered her voice and mouthed over the children's heads – 'Mrs Potts from three doors down has done a Christmas stocking each for the bairns.' Resuming her normal tone, she added, 'Mick'll bring them with the turkey. An' I did you a Christmas cake when I made mine.'

Again she pointed, this time to the table where in the midst of the collection of food reposed a small fruit cake, iced and decorated with a sprig of holly. 'Oh, an' Mrs Irvin, her with the twins, has sent a bag of clothes for Harry that hers have grown out of.'

Blindly, Kate reached out and sat down as her legs gave way. The hard lump in her chest, hidden deep within her heart – the lump that had been with her throughout her childhood in the workhouse but which had gathered weight after the last conversation with the matron – was beginning to melt, forcing its way upwards into her throat. Gasping at the strength of it, she tried to speak but failed, the tears raining from her eyes as she choked against the flood.

'There, there, hinny, don't take on so.' Mrs Kirby had risen with Rebecca in her arms and come to pat her awkwardly on the shoulder. 'We all know what a struggle you've had, an' you such a good mam to them two bairns. It's Christmas, lass, an' if we can't look out for each other then, it's a poor do.'

As Mrs Kirby had been speaking Harry had climbed off his chair and was now standing at his mother's knee. Kate raised her head to look at her son through her streaming eyes and saw his bottom lip trembling at the sight of her in tears. Reaching out, she pulled him to her and managed to murmur, 'It's all right, my precious. It's all right. I'm crying 'cos I'm happy.'

Harry stared at his mother and then up at Mrs Kirby, who had a tear trickling down her cheek. His small brow creased. 'What do you do when you're sad?' he asked, a wealth of bewilderment in his voice.

Matthew Wood had never considered himself an emotional type of individual – not until the first time he had set eyes on Kate, anyway. He remembered every detail of that afternoon – the fresh heady smell of spring sweetening the air, the vivid cornflower blue of the sky dotted with cotton-wool clouds, and Kate. Bonny, painfully shy Kate. The impact of her had been like a punch in the solar plexus, but whereas one could recover from a physical blow, this had been different. There had been no way to recover from the ache and pain of Kate not knowing he existed. Oh, she'd been civil enough; she'd even smiled at his jokes now and again, but no matter how outrageous his efforts to get her to notice him, he hadn't been able to get past that aloof, distant air of hers. His only comfort had been that she treated every lad in their crowd the same.

He took off his cap, which was covered in snow, banging it on his trouser leg before pulling it on again.

Then had come the announcement of war and he'd known he had to let her know how he felt about her before he left for France. There had been no rhyme or reason to the compulsion, in view of her indifference; he'd just known that he couldn't leave England's shores without making himself plain. And so he'd gone to see her at her place of work, quaking in his boots. And she'd been unlike the Kate he knew – softer, somehow. It had given him the courage to ask her to write to him, but with the damn cook eyeing them from the window and Kate all of a dither, he hadn't said the words burning on his tongue. That he loved her, that he would always love her till his dying day.

But he had kissed her and she hadn't pulled away,

and that had been enough then. He'd told himself his letters would convey all that he hadn't said. He hadn't bargained on being taken prisoner within days of landing in France.

He shook his head as the bloodbath that had been Mons seared his memory. British troops had fought alongside their French and Belgian comrades in a bitter struggle for the town, and for the first time in his life he had seen the anatomy of his fellow man laid bare as German bayonets and machine guns had done their grisly work. He'd been badly injured and near death for a long time; ironically it had been the expertise of a German doctor that had eventually enabled him to pull through.

It was only then he'd discovered his parents had been sent a telegram in error reporting his demise.

He stubbed out his cigarette butt and straightened from where he'd been leaning against a house wall on the opposite side of the road to Kate's front door.

Had she married Timothy Finlay because she loved him? Would she still have married someone else if he hadn't been injured and had written the letters telling her he loved her? She had been as cold as ice when he'd seen her at the funeral, her manner making it abundantly clear she wanted none of him, even as a friend. That had hurt, and at the time it had seemed answer enough, but over the last months he had wondered if it was grief at Tim's passing that made her act that way. After all, she'd buried her husband that very day.

Or was he clutching at straws? He hunched his shoulders, ashamed of the weakness in him that was Kate, a weakness he managed to throttle during the day when he was working on the farm but which came to torment him each night.

He was a prosperous farmer now; as an only child his parents' passing had meant the farm came to him lock, stock and barrel, but it didn't mean anything. *Not without her.*

Matthew gave himself a mental shake. There were plenty more fish in the sea. What was he doing pining after a lass who had upped and married someone else and who had a couple of bairns to prove it? He was barmy, that was the truth of it, and what the hell he was doing standing out in the dark on Christmas Eve in the bitter cold, he didn't know. He could be back at the farmhouse in front of a roaring fire with a glass of brandy warming his bones. He'd had more than one offer from lassies hereabouts to warm his bed an' all. He smiled grimly. There was nothing like prosperity to put a come-hither sparkle in a lass's eye.

He took off his cap once more, slapping it against his leg and then irritably stuffing it back on his head. Enough of this foolishness, standing here like a lovesick lad wet behind the ears. He didn't dare to think what his farmhands would say if they could see him.

He should go home.

The food had been put away, the paper chains were hanging gaily across the kitchen ceiling and for once the kitchen was as warm as toast; there was even a small fire taking the chill off the front room where Harry and Rebecca were fast asleep. Ellie had come in and watched the children while Kate had returned to Mrs Bell's to collect her two shillings. At least she had money in the pot for the rent man now. Not much, admittedly, but if she eked out the coal and the food she might be able to put all the money she earned next week into the pot too. Enough to pay two or three weeks off the back rent, anyway.

She refused to think about the weeks after that; it was Christmas Eve and there was magic in the air and she didn't want to spoil it by facing reality. Not tonight. Not this one special night.

She glanced around the kitchen, mellow and cosy in the glow from the fire in the range and the dim light from the oil lamp in the middle of the table. The battered old furniture had taken on a grace it could never aspire to in the harsh light of day, and even the snow falling thickly outside the window seemed pretty tonight, rather than just another obstacle to be overcome.

Once Mick had brought the turkey and the stockings for Harry and Rebecca she would go to bed, she told herself tiredly, and, as if in answer to the thought, there was a knock at the door.

Her brow wrinkled. What on earth was Mick doing knocking on the front door rather than coming in as usual by the back yard? No one used the front door apart from the doctor or Reverend Alridge, and the latter had only come to the house once, to finalize the arrangements for Timothy's funeral. Perhaps it was the doctor for Mr or Mrs Gilbert upstairs, but she would have thought they'd have told her if one of them was poorly and expecting Dr Clark.

When she opened the door she stared at the snow-covered figure standing on the pavement. For a moment time stood still, and then deep inside her body a trembling began and a whirling, frantic cacophony of thoughts.

'Hello, Kate,' Matthew said softly.

She tried to pull herself together, but coming on top of the emotion of the last hours it was beyond her.

He waited a moment and then cleared his throat, a nervous sound, and strangely it restored her equilibrium long enough for her to say shakily, 'Matthew. What a surprise.'

'Can I come in for a moment?'

'What? Oh, yes. Yes, of course. I'm sorry, I wasn't expecting anyone . . .' Her voice trailed away as she realized she was babbling. She stood aside for him to step into the hall. 'Go along to the kitchen, the bairns are asleep in the front room.'

Her legs were weak as she followed him and when he turned to face her, his tall broad figure in its heavy overcoat filled her vision to the exclusion of anything else. Willing her voice not to tremble, she said with a composure she was proud of in the circumstances, 'What brings you out on such a snowy night?'

He hesitated, then simply said, 'You.'

'Me?'

'I was going to say all sorts of things if you answered the door. That I was passing, that I felt Tim would expect his old friends to make sure you were doing all right, that . . .' He shook his head, rubbing his hand across his face. 'That I hoped we could be friends. And I do still hope that,' he added quickly. 'But now you're in front of me and I can't pretend. The truth is, I need to spell out how I feel about you, for my sanity if nothing else. Kate, I love you. I've always loved you and I shall go on loving you to my dying day. I've come to realize it's something I can't do anything about. You're here—' he touched a hand to his chest – 'in the heart and soul of me, and I know it's too soon after Tim, but I need to know if there is any hope at all for me in the future. I'll wait. I'll wait forever if that's what you want, but I can't carry on not knowing, and tonight, Christmas Eve—' he rubbed his face again – 'I suppose I was hoping for a miracle.'

She stared at him, a change coming over her face and the guarded, wary expression melting at the look in his eyes.

Emboldened, he murmured, 'I thought – that day I came to see you before I went to France – I thought you might care for me a little?'

'I did.' Her voice a whisper, she breathed, 'I do.'

The dropping of her defences was too much for him to take in for a moment. Then he reached out, pulling her into his arms.

This time the kiss was not the swift, tentative one of a nervous suitor but that of a man hungry for the woman he had been waiting for. Their lips clinging and their bodies pressed as if to merge, they stood for endless moments in the dimly lit room, lost in their own heady world.

When at last Matthew raised his head, it was to murmur, shakily, 'Kate, will you marry me quickly? As soon as I can arrange things? I want to take care of you and the bairns and there's no need for us to wait . . . is there?'

It would cause a stir, with Timothy not having been gone a full year. There would be gossip, and every busybody hereabouts nattering to their neighbours over the walls dividing their back yards, relishing the whiff of a scandal. There would be those who would declare they'd suspected she had been carrying-on for some time, and she would be labelled a bad lot.

For a moment the old fears were strong, and then Kate looked into Matthew's face. This was *her* miracle, not Harry's or Rebecca's – not even Matthew's – and she had to grasp it with both hands and believe in what she had been given by One who loved her, just as she was. And she took the first step towards the confident, happy woman she was destined to become, lifting her hand to tenderly stroke his cheek as she smiled.

'No, there's no need to wait at all.'

A Christmas Tradition in the Bradshaw Household

RITA BRADSHAW

A Christmas tradition in our household is the Christmas Eve walk with the dogs. No matter the weather or the amount of work to be done, Christmas Eve afternoon will see us taking the dogs to the nearby woods and letting them have a whale of a time. The afternoon is theirs, and humans have to fit in!

It's often cold and icy, sometimes frosty or snowy, and to walk home as the sun sets in the crisp air with tired, satisfied furry babies means that Christmas has begun. They have an extra-special tasty dinner and then curl up on the settee with us (I know! Dogs on the furniture! Sorry, but we don't care!) while we have a glass of wine and watch TV with the lights twinkling on the Christmas tree.

Magic!

The Gift

Margaret Dickinson

CHRISTMAS EVE, 1914

The sound echoed eerily across the frozen waste they called No Man's Land.

'They're singing,' Tom whispered to the man standing beside him in the trench.

'In German,' Joe whispered back. 'The Hun is singing Silent Night.'

'How d'you know that?'

'I know the tune. We sing it in church at home.'

'I've never heard it before.'

The two men were quiet now, listening to the deep, melodious voices. And their own thoughts turned to those at home. Mary would be helping their three children hang up their stockings near the fireplace, Tom thought. Then they would kiss the picture of him, each one in turn – she had told him this in her last letter –

before climbing the stairs and snuggling down in bed. Then she would fill their stockings with whatever little gifts she had been able to afford, no doubt shedding a tear because he wasn't there to help her. Tom swallowed the lump that rose in his throat. He hoped she'd remember to put a shiny new penny in the toe of each stocking.

'I've hidden them in my drawer,' he'd told her. 'Don't forget now.' They'd been the last words he'd said to her before he'd marched away, a proud volunteer to take the King's Shilling and fight for his country.

Joe was thinking of his widowed mother. His three younger brothers were itching to follow his example and enlist. But Joe wasn't sure it was a good idea, not now he had seen the conditions out here. If they should all be killed, their mother would have no one. After Christmas, he promised himself – the Christmas by which everyone had believed the war would be over – he would write to each one and warn them . . .

'They can sing. I'll give 'em that,' Tom murmured. Cautiously, he started to stand up, to look above the parapet, just to see . . .

Joe grabbed his arm and pulled him back. 'Keep down, you fool. It'll be a trap.'

Now they could hear others close by, in their own trench, whispering. The hymn came to an end and the silence was even more unnerving than the singing had been. And then, spontaneous applause broke out in the British trenches with cries of 'Bravo' and 'Happy Christmas'.

Rising above the noise and the laughter, they heard a German shouting, 'Tommy? Tommy? Can you hear me, Tommy? Happy Christmas, Tommy.'

'He knows my name!' Tom's voice rose in panic. 'How's he know my name?'

'He doesn't, you idiot,' Joe laughed. 'It's what the Hun call us. We're "Tommies" to them, just like they're "The Hun" to us.'

'Yeah, but we can't shout that to him. Not if he's trying to be friendly. It's an insult.'

'Friendly? More likely he wants to shoot your head off the minute you pop up above the parapet.'

'I thought we called 'em "Fritz".'

'Well – yes – that too.'

'That's not rude, is it?'

'I don't suppose so, no.'

Tentatively, Tom lifted his head. 'What do you want, Fritz?'

'Ha! You are there!'

'Of course we're here,' Tom muttered. 'Where does he think we are? We're here and they're there – more's the pity.'

This wasn't the glorious war Tom had envisaged when he'd marched away with the cheers of the townsfolk ringing in his ears and urging him on. He was cold and hungry and his feet never seemed to be dry. There was the constant fear of being shot or blown to smithereens, to say nothing of sharing his dugout with cat-sized rats. And yet, he'd made some good pals. Joe, here beside him, for one. But now, it seemed, someone from the other side wanted to be friendly.

'I have present for you, Tommy.' The German was shouting again.

'I bet he has,' Joe muttered morosely. 'A bullet through the head, most likely. Throw him one of your jam-tin grenades, Tom.'

Tom was poking his head cautiously above the parapet again. Then he ducked down quickly. 'He's walking towards us carrying some sort of light.' There was a pause whilst Tom took another quick peek. 'There's loads of 'em climbing out of their trench and coming towards us.'

'Are they all carrying lights?'

'No, but I can see their shapes.' More voices filled the night air, German and British mingling in mutual greeting.

There was movement in their own trench now and, glancing to their left, the two men saw that some of their compatriots were climbing the ladders and going over the top of the parapet. But it wasn't the usual 'over the top' order signalled by a whistle when the soldiers launched themselves, guns at the ready, towards No

Man's Land and on, through a hail of bullets, towards the enemy trenches.

'Look! Just look. Some of our lads are going to meet them,' Tom said.

'Idiots! They'll get killed – or court-martialled. Have they forgotten the order that came down the lines only yesterday? No fraternizing with the enemy, it said. The top brass must have been expecting something like this to happen.'

'Joe – he's here – the one with the light,' Tom whispered urgently. 'He's standing right above us.'

They both looked up to see the grinning German soldier in his heavy trench coat and spiked helmet, standing on the parapet of the British trench and holding a small Christmas tree with six tiny flickering candles. He was a big man, tall and broad-shouldered, and he had a thick, curving moustache.

'I bring you gift for Christmas, Tommy,' the German said in thick, guttural English. 'Ha-ha.' He laughed raucously, the sound carrying through the darkness. 'We are not going to fight you tomorrow. We play games together. Football, yes? My friend, he has a football.'

'Is he serious?' Joe muttered. 'Who the heck brings a football to war with 'em?'

'Evidently, a German.'

All along the British trench now, soldiers were climbing out to meet the men whom only a few hours earlier they had been trying to kill. Making a sudden decision, Tom grasped the ladder, put his foot on the bottom rung and heaved himself up, leaving his gun leaning against the wall of the trench, not wanted or needed in this strange, impromptu truce. With a shrug of resignation, Joe followed him and as they climbed out of their trench, very slowly and a little fearfully, a wondrous sight met their eyes. As far as they could see in both directions, small, candlelit Christmas trees were set on top of the German parapets, flickering and glinting on the frosty earth. The two men stood for a moment, staring about them as soldiers from both sides appeared, like rabbits from a warren, and walked towards one another.

Tom turned and held out his hand to the German. 'How do you do, Fritz?' he murmured, prompting another bark of laughter from the stranger.

'My name is Kurt – Kurt Schulze.'

'And mine's Tom Benson.'

'Ha – you really are "Tommy".'

The German grasped Tom's hand in a warm, firm handshake and the Englishman winced. 'By heck, he's got a grip of iron,' he muttered. 'I wouldn't like that round my throat. I wonder if he's learned unarmed combat, an' all.'

'I expect so,' Joe murmured.

'Yes – yes, I am,' Tom said, loudly, 'and this is Joe.'

The introductions made, the three men stood awkwardly for a moment, unsure how to strike up a real conversation, until the German thrust the little Christmas tree into Tom's hand. 'There, you take. Put it in your trench when you eat your turkey. Ha-ha.'

'Fat chance of such luxury,' Joe said, but his initial reluctance was thawing a little now; this German seemed genuine, and beside them, all along the line, soldiers from opposite sides were laughing and talking together, offering each other cigarettes and chocolate.

Joe and Tom had arrived only recently in the front line, just west of Ploegsteert Wood, which the Tommies soon nicknamed 'Plugstreet Wood'. They were among the first of Kitchener's volunteers to replace the battle-weary and, by this time, the much-depleted British Expeditionary Force's battalions. They hadn't seen the battle at Mons, where the British had been forced to retreat, losing a lot of the ground they had occupied, or the fighting near the river Marne, which had been more successful for their side. They hadn't been there in the middle of September when both the French and the British Commanders had given the order to their troops to entrench. Deep, winding trenches had been dug and were still being dug when Tom and Joe arrived.

'I didn't know this is what we'd have to do,' Joe had grumbled, as he'd tried to deepen the already waterlogged trench. 'Looks like we should be issued with spades, not rifles.'

'Keep your head down, mate, and stop moaning,' Tom had warned. He was relieved that there was no shelling at that time, though they had to be careful of snipers. Already they had seen one of their comrades killed by a single shot as he'd stood up to ease his aching back.

'I wonder what he's like,' Tom had mused as they worked side by side.

'Who?'

'The Hun. I mean, is he really the barbarian the papers have been making out?'

'I wouldn't think so for a minute. He'll be much the same as us, I shouldn't wonder. He'll have parents and wives, mebbe children even. He just speaks a different language, that's all.'

'But they hate us, don't they?'

'So the papers say, but isn't it what they call "propaganda"?

'What's that?'

'Stories put about deliberately to make us hate the enemy.' Joe seemed a little more knowledgeable than Tom. 'Mind you, he does look a bit of a comic figure strutting about in his spiked helmet.'

'Mebbe we look as daft in our puttees.'

'Aye, and a fat lot of good they are against this mud.'

Three days before Christmas, the rain had stopped and the trenches began to dry out a little, but then came snow.

'This'll be worse still,' Joe had groaned. 'What we need is a good, hard frost.'

Joe got his wish on Christmas Eve. The digging in their section stopped as hard ground replaced the squelching mud. 'Someone's got a guardian angel up there looking out for us,' Tom laughed. 'This is a welcome Christmas present: no digging. And it's a beautiful winter's day. Just look at the frost coating everything, Joe, sparkling in the sunshine. I couldn't have decorated the landscape better than Nature has done.'

'That's all very well, Tom, but it's good sniping weather. I'd sooner have a bit of fog.'

And now Tom and Joe were standing close to a real, live Hun. But he didn't look like a barbarian. He looked rather jovial and friendly, Tom thought as he stretched out his hand to receive the lit-up Christmas tree. 'Thanks, Fritz – I mean, Kurt.' Suddenly, the enemy had a human face, a name; now he was a real person to the British Tommy.

'Wait, I have a present for *you*.' Tom turned and re-treated down the ladder into his own trench, carrying the little tree, the candles flickering and threatening to go out, but he carried it carefully, anxious not to let the German think he didn't value the gift. He set it on top of their own parapet and then hurried to the dugout he and Joe used and returned to the ladder holding the Christmas pudding Mary had sent.

'It is from my wife,' Tom told him as he handed it to Kurt. 'She made it herself.'

'Ah, that is a wonderful gift. I will share it with my friend, yes?'

Tom nodded, still watching the German closely. They had been warned by their superiors to be extra vigilant at Christmas. 'The enemy may attack us when he thinks we are relaxed and celebrating.'

Was all this still a devious trap? Tom was thinking even as he handed over the present. But Kurt was clutching it to his chest as if it was the most precious thing he had ever been given. 'Tomorrow, I bring you beer.'

'Beer?' Tom and Joe replied together in surprise.

'Ha – yes. There is brewery behind the line. You haven't bombed it yet. Ha-ha.' His laughter echoed once again through the frosty night air.

The two Englishmen smiled at each other. Real beer; they couldn't wait.

'I go back now,' Kurt said, 'but I see you tomorrow. I bring my friend and we play football, yes?'

Tom and Joe watched him all the way back to his own trench and only when Kurt had disappeared below the German parapet did they turn and climb back down their own ladder. All along the line, the British soldiers, returning to their dugouts, were marvelling at what had happened.

'Look what one of 'em's given me.' A youth, barely

older than sixteen, held several cigarettes in the palm of his hand. 'I felt bad, because I hadn't anything to give him.'

'Ne'er mind, mate. Tomorrow you can give him some of those sweets your mam sent you. That's if you haven't eaten them all by now,' replied Tom.

'D'you think they'll come back tomorrow?'

'I hope so,' Joe said. 'That chap we were talking to's promised to bring us a barrel of beer.' Joe's change of heart had been sudden and complete.

For the next hour, singing sounded from both trenches. First the British gave a hearty rendition of 'It's a long way to Tipperary' and then the Germans sang one of their favourite songs. Both sides ended the night as if in tacit agreement by singing the same carol, 'Oh Come All Ye Faithful', together but in different languages.

As the singing died away and both sides applauded each other, the night ended with shouts of 'Happy Christmas, Englander' and 'See you tomorrow, Fritz'. Tom and Joe turned to their sandbagged dugout.

'Did all that really happen?' Joe said, shaking his head in disbelief. 'I reckon I've been dreaming.'

'Takes some believing,' Tom agreed, as they settled down to try to get a little sleep in the bitter cold of their shelter. 'We'll see what tomorrow brings, eh?'

'Aye,' Joe said, some of his pessimism returning. 'Mebbe they'll be shooting at us again by then.'

The following morning, after breakfast and prayers, Tom and Joe heard Kurt's loud voice. 'Hey Tommy, are you there?' This time, Joe did not chide Tom when he poked his head above the parapet.

'Happy Christmas, Kurt.'

'Ha! Happy Christmas, Tommy. We play football, yes? I have the ball.'

'Righto,' Tom called back and he and Joe climbed out of the trench. Along both the trenches more men climbed out, and soon there was a football match in progress. More and more soldiers lined the edges of No Man's Land watching and cheering on their own side.

'It's a pity, y'know,' Joe said, as they returned to their trench after the match, breathless yet exhilarated even though the Germans had been victorious with a score of three to two, 'that this whole shenanigans can't be settled on a football pitch.'

Tom laughed wryly. 'But they won, Joe. We can't have that.'

'Aye, and they might win the war, an' all,' Joe muttered morosely.

'Aw, mate, don't let anyone else hear you talking like that. You could be put up against a wall and shot by our own side. Anyway, guess what? Kurt was telling me he's a barber by trade. He's going to cut my hair this afternoon.'

'Really? I could do with a trim myself.'

Later that day, Kurt had a queue for his makeshift barber's shop, set up in the middle of No Man's Land. Someone from the German side had produced a chair and Kurt brandished his scissors with relish. 'I brought the tools of my trade to war with me,' he said. 'I would never go anywhere without them.'

'What's he charging?' Joe asked as they stood in line.

'Five fags or an ounce of baccy,' Tom replied promptly as they watched the professional at work. 'And just look at him – that's the best haircut I've seen since I left home. Not like the army barbers, is he?'

'Call them barbers? I've seen a better job done by a sheep shearer,' Joe muttered scathingly. 'The one that did me when I volunteered nearly had me ear off.'

'You know, when I write and tell Mary about this, she'll never believe me.'

'None of 'em will back home. We're here to win a war, not be playing footer and having our hair cut in the middle of No Man's Land by the enemy.'

Tom glanced around him at the groups of soldiers, listening to the laughter and chatter as they drank beer from the barrels which the Germans had rolled across that morning, and watching as the men from both sides exchanged small gifts. Someone was playing a penny whistle – and a group of soldiers were singing, each side trying to teach the other their favourite songs amidst much hilarity at the mangling of their respective languages.

When the queue for Kurt's ministrations had all gone and there was only Tom left to do, the Englishman pulled a photograph out of his pocket as he sat down in the chair. 'This is my Mary, Kurt, and my three children.'

The German took the picture and stared down at it for a long time before handing it back to Tom. There were tears in the big man's eyes. 'You have a wonderful family, Tommy. I hope you live to get back to them. Now, sir, how would you like your hair cut today?'

'Short back and sides, my man, if you please.' And the two men laughed together.

As night fell on the strange Christmas Day, the two sides parted company with much backslapping and promises to meet again in the morning. On Boxing Day, they might be able to repeat the camaraderie of today, but after that . . .

'Kurt – I have a gift for you. Wait a moment . . .'

Tom hurried back to the British trench, climbed down the ladder and stumbled to the dugout he shared with Joe. Amongst his possessions he found what he was looking for. Returning to the waiting German he said, 'I want you to have this. It's what Princess Mary has sent to every soldier. She's the daughter of our King, you know.'

He held out the metal box with the Princess's likeness and the date 'Christmas 1914' stamped on the lid. Almost reverently, Kurt opened it. Inside was a packet of cigarettes, a pipe and tobacco and a card which read, *'With Best Wishes for a Happy Christmas and a Victorious New Year, From The Princess Mary and Friends at Home'*.

Kurt gave a bark of laughter as he handed the card back to Tom. 'I think she means this for you, but I will accept the gift gratefully. Thank you, my friend.' Clutching the box, he turned away abruptly and called back over his shoulder, 'I will see you tomorrow.'

'That was a bit sudden, wasn't it?' Joe said, staring after the figure disappearing into the gloom.

'Aye, it was, but didn't you notice?'

'Notice what?'

'I reckon he had tears in his eyes.'

'Don't be daft,' Joe scoffed. 'A big German like that getting soppy over a few ciggies and a bit of baccy. Come on, let's get back and see what muck they've cooked up for us tonight.'

But their main meal that Christmas Day was a feast.

Parcels from home had been opened and shared and there was tinned turkey, Christmas pudding and rich fruitcake, to say nothing of biscuits and sweets, for everyone.

Once again, the sound of singing from both trenches filled the darkness, yet tonight there was a more sombre note to their voices and Tom felt tears fill his own eyes as he thought about Mary and his children and wondered what they were doing at this moment. Never mind what Joe said, Tom was sure he'd seen tears in the big German's eyes too.

Kurt was at the top of their ladder early the next morning. 'Tommy, Tommy, I have a gift for you. Come out here.'

Tom emerged from the dugout to see the big German standing on the edge of the parapet beckoning him. He climbed up and stood beside him as Kurt thrust a small, flat silver cigarette case into his hand. 'I want you to have this.'

'Oh Kurt, I couldn't, mate.' He looked down at it, turning it over in his hands. 'You can't give me this. It's far too expensive. Besides, it's got your initials engraved on it.'

'So,' Kurt grinned. 'It is mine to give, yes?'

'Well – I suppose so.'

'You will always remember me.'

'Of course I will.'

'And now we play footer again and we beat you again, yes?'

'Uh-oh, not this time, big feller.' Tom shook his head as he slipped the cigarette case into the breast pocket of his jacket. 'This time *we* win, yes? Joe – round up the lads, we've got a return match . . .'

As darkness gathered, an air of sadness settled over the soldiers on both sides of the barbed wire. They all knew – British soldiers and Germans alike – that the brief period of fraternization was over. The killing would have to begin again. But it would be hard to fire their guns knowing that they were perhaps killing the very man with whom only hours before they'd shared a mug of beer, or smoked a cigarette or shown their precious photographs. It would be heartbreaking to hear the shells fired and see earth blown high into the air, taking bodies with it. On both sides, there would be regret.

Tom was reluctant to fire a shot, but he knew if he was caught aiming into the air or refusing to go 'over the top' he would face a court martial and would probably be shot for cowardice, desertion or both. So, he had no choice. After a sprinkling of snow on Boxing Day that turned to sleet and then to rain, the trenches and surrounding areas were soon back to their muddy, waterlogged state. The daily battle with the cold and wet was uppermost in all their minds. Tom and Joe were amongst those relieved from their duties at the front and they returned to their billets behind the lines for rest and recuperation. But the whisper amongst the soldiers was that the 'truce' seemed to be lingering. Both sets of opponents seemed reluctant to fire on their new-found friends, no doubt with the strong disapproval of the 'top brass' on each side. There was little real fighting until the middle of March when Tom and Joe found themselves back in the thick of a battle near Neuve Chappelle. Memories of the Christmas festivities faded and the war was once again a cruel reality. Yet Tom still carried the silver cigarette case in his breast pocket. Side by side, he and Joe obeyed the commands of their superiors; daily they carried out their duties, longing for rest, yearning for it all to be over, praying that they would not get killed . . .

Tom wasn't expecting it when a lone sniper's bullet hit him, swiftly followed by another. He felt the thud against the left-hand side of his chest that knocked the wind from him. He put up his hand to the place and the second shot penetrated his hand and embedded itself in his shoulder. He fell back with a gasp, his only thought the unfinished letter to his beloved Mary.

'Tom! Tom!' He heard Joe's frantic voice as the other man pulled him up out of the water in the bottom of the trench. And then, for Tom, everything went black.

He came to in a field hospital just behind their lines and Joe was still with him, talking to him, crying and laughing all in the same breath. 'You lucky so-and-so, Tom Benson. You've got a Blighty wound. You're going home. The bullet that would have killed you, hit that cigarette case in your pocket. Old Kurt saved your life, mate.'

Tom Benson returned to Mary and his children and for the rest of his life he carried the silver cigarette case in his breast pocket. From time to time, he would take it out, turn it over and over in his hands and trace with his finger the dent between the K and the S that the bullet had made. And he never tired of telling his children and his grandchildren the story of how a simple gift from an enemy soldier in the middle of a terrible war had given him the rest of his life.

Christmas at Thalstead Halt

Annie Murray

There was already a promise of snow in the air as I stepped outside that morning. The sky hung heavy over the woods and there was a quiet feeling of expectation. It was an atmosphere most fitting as we awaited the birth of Our Lord – and for that night which, though I did not know it then, was to prove the strangest and most wondrous of my life.

It was 23rd December 1886, many years ago now, before the turn of the new century and the more modern world in which we lately find ourselves. I was then a young man of twenty-seven years, and by this tender age I had attained the position of stationmaster at Thalstead. While we were called a 'halt' – the village being a mile away to the east – we ran a proper station in this humble place. I saw how they trusted me as a sober and upright appointment, devoted servant as I was both to the laws of God and to the commerce of the Great Western Railway. Hence I was granted a home in the station cottage. To my great joy I could thus also give a home to my mother, Grace Lee, who had been a struggling widow since only months after my birth. Both of us rejoiced in this good fortune.

As I stepped toward the woods with my axe to gather fuel, I felt the first flakes like cold feathers against my cheeks. By the time I returned, the sack heavy on my shoulder, the air was awhirl with white, my boots leaving tracks behind me. I laid most of the fuel in the old sty behind the house and carried inside enough for our needs.

'It's coming down all right,' I said to Mother. 'We look set for a white Christmas.'

Mother, then close to fifty years, a woman rosy and sweet of face, was my comfort and companion, as she had been from my infancy. I was a sensitive child. It was always she who put my world to rights after the teasing of other boys; she who fed me, kept me safe from the world's snares and taught me my prayers. She was always there, with her hair caught and pinned in a bun, an apron on. And if that hair had begun to show frosting like the snow outside, I barely paid it heed. I saw her so often I did not note the changes.

'It's lovely,' she said, as she stirred our porridge on the fire. Over its more mundane smell rose the rich, spicy scents of mincemeat. Our cottage was brick-floored and simple. 'Though it'd better stop. We don't want it getting too deep – an icing on the hills would be a pretty sight, though!'

She was ever kind to me, my dear little mother, though I know she worried about our isolation here.

'You are at the age when you should be finding a nice wife for yourself, Thomas,' she would say sometimes, a sad light in her eyes. 'Not mouldering away here with an old woman like me.'

'If the Lord wishes it, it will happen in time,' I would say to her lightly. But in my heart I doubted it. I did not see myself as the marrying kind. My Bible reading and catechism had made me wary of the opposite sex: in truth they frightened me. And I had learned to mistrust the lusts of the flesh, guarding myself against such gross excitement. I turned my energies to godly work. Should stirrings of a carnal nature disturb me, I banished them sternly with dry thoughts and strenuous work. Besides, when, in this isolated life we lived, was I ever sufficiently abroad in society to meet any young woman?

The train passed through Thalstead three times a day in each direction along the single track, between the junction at ——— and the coast. On this day, so close to Christmas, the morning passed in a flurry of activity. Myself, my assistant and the station porter were much occupied in unloading a season-rich assortment of kegs and barrels, sprays of greenery, live fowls and sacks of vegetables, and carting them onward to the villages. Our breath wreathed the cold air. The carriages were pressed full of those travelling to where they would reside for the season, in hope of warm welcomes and hearths, of jollity and full bellies. At moments, imagining their festive days to follow, I envied them their social advantages. But I rebuked myself, counted the many blessings of my life and put an end to such ungrateful folly.

All day, around and betwixt the busyness of engine and whistle, of rumbling barrows, the snort and clatter of the horses and the hen-coop chatter of voices, the snow fell in dense flakes. While we talked of there soon being an end to it, it rather thickened to a whirling blizzard so that the vista before us was obscured by a wall of white. It was as much as I could do to make out the station building with its adjacent waiting room, and our cottage close by. The rails shrank ahead into nothingness, in the grey gloom of the afternoon and the sheltering woods.

Before dark, I bade the other men make for home. I would manage the last train back through alone, for I knew that the traffic from it would be lighter. Without much reluctance, the two of them agreed.

'So long, old lad!' one cried as they set off – joking, as he was several years my senior. 'Go steady, now!'

'Don't you be getting up to any mischief, will you, Believing Thomas?' said the other.

'Goodnight!' I called, as their laughter faded from me. I felt a moment of doubt at their teasing. But I told myself that they took me for a good fellow, with all my sober ways.

The snow still did not abate but rather came on stronger. I watched it build upon the wood and along the tracks, high as a man's thigh. The last train from the coast was due to reach Thalstead by 4.20 p.m., but the time came and went and the darkness gathered thickly.

I paced the platform, my peaked cap small refuge from the blundering flakes. Darkness was all about us now and the dim lights of the station reduced it to an oasis, marooned in an obscured land. I was freezing cold and took refuge inside our cottage: another world, warm and lit, and full of the smells of chopped onion and spiced pies fresh from the oven. It was approaching five o'clock.

'I'm worried, Mother,' I said. 'Where can they be?'

'Is there no word?' she asked. Our eyes met, imagining the two carriages and guard's van stranded behind their engine, out in the murk.

I shook my head. 'The wire has been dead all afternoon.'

The best part of another hour passed. We drank tea and waited. My innards tightened ever more with worry.

At length Mother stopped in her work and held up a finger. 'Listen – there it is.'

I leapt up, hearing the faintest whistle of a train, and ran out to see a dot of light inching closer at not much more than walking pace. With a low chugging, the orange sparks from the furnace whirling upwards and the softly lit windows lighting up the night, it edged its way along the platform and stopped with a long hiss of steam. From one of the carriages I heard, I thought, the sounds of a woman in the throes of hysterics.

'Thomas – you there?' the engine driver hailed me.

'Here!' I cried. I knew Percy Rogers well, for he passed through several times each day, as did his crew, fireman Bob Rimes and guard Ernie Brooks, a proud team of fellows. Percy leaned out, pulling his cap over his face.

'Reckon we can't go on,' he said, nodding with an air of doom at the track ahead. 'We're here for the night, Thomas.' He looked along the train. 'There's only a handful aboard. Reckon you and your mother can manage us?'

'Of course,' I said, already resolved to rise to this occasion. 'Bring them along.' And I ran towards the house, crying, 'Mother!'

They climbed down from the now dark carriages, the shrieks of the hysterical woman and the soothing voices of others strangely loud above their muffled footsteps and the whirling snow. There came another male voice, most loud and booming.

'I must have my trunk – that's it, help me lift it!'

Bob Rimes the fireman appeared, bent over and rolling something along in front of him. 'We'll make up the fire in the waiting room,' he said. 'Us lads'll settle well in there.'

'Ah – do let me accompany you!' A face loomed out of the gloom, pale between hat and clerical clothing, with a blond moustache. 'I am Cecil Walmsley, Vicar of St Simeon's in ———. I am more than happy to accompany these good fellows into the waiting room and learn from them the lore of the railway. This—' he extended an arm towards the train – 'is a Prairie tank engine, is it not?'

As Bob Rimes straightened up, saying, 'Oh, now, Reverend, I think you'd be better off going into the house with Mr Lee . . .' I saw three women in bonnets and shawls emerge from the train, one snivelling loudly, a second timidly seeking to give solace. Behind them limped a younger girl in a much plainer bonnet, her head bowed against the weather. She was of slender build, the most marked thing I could see of her then being the awkwardness of her gait, her lilting somewhat to one side with every step. I felt the beat of nervousness inside me. I had not reckoned on all this.

'Oh no, truly!' the cleric was protesting. 'It would be a delight to accompany you gentlemen. I am, if nothing else, a man of the people!'

'Might as well let 'im,' Percy instructed. 'We'll leave Ernie to sort out Captain Blood over there.' He nodded towards the man with the booming voice. He was a tall, perilously thin-looking fellow with a host of dark, dis-orderly whiskers and was fussing about with something at the door to the guard's van.

'Come along, my dears – come inside and welcome.' I was calmed by the voice of my mother once again, as she stood wrapped in her coat and shawl, ushering the group of gentlewomen into the house. As I had done so many times in my life, I gave thanks to God for her kindly ways.

Inside, we took in the size of our unexpected party. The train crew, along with the eager clergyman and two other young men from the carriages, were all assembled in the waiting room. On visiting them with fuel for the fire and to assure them that we should shortly bring them food, I found them with the lamps lit and the fire burning nicely. They were all lounging along the benches, except for the reverend gentleman who sat leaning forward, asking eager questions. From the tail of my eye I saw that Percy already had a barrel laid along one bench, and I discerned that they were intending to make free with this plunder from the train. I steadfastly ignored it, not wanting to acknowledge such surrender to the vagaries of temptation. In this atmosphere of un-bridled male licence, I found myself torn asunder by the desire to escape to the refuge of my house, while in great trepidation as to the exact nature of the females I might encounter there.

'Off you go, St Thomas,' Percy Rogers said, with in-dulgent mockery. 'You don't need to trouble yourself with us. You go and see to the ladies.'

I retired, a little stung, amid their scattered laughter. As I entered our house out of the dark and cold, my eyes adjusted to the cosy scene within. My mother, bless her soul, had already made the assembled company com-fortable, the distressed lady seemed to have calmed her-self and order was restored. They were settled about the room, the women's bonnets laid aside, and the only strange obstruction I noticed was a large black object deposited in front of the fire.

'Ah, Thomas!' My mother's voice rang with pride. 'This is my son, Thomas Lee, stationmaster here,' she said. 'We are happy to accommodate you in this adverse weather, aren't we, Tom?'

'We are,' I said. Looking about me, I perceived that the entire company before me was female, apart from the tall bewhiskered gentleman. His mature years, tight black trousers and fusty jacket put me in mind of the Prince Consort, if His Royal Highness had perhaps spent several nights at large sleeping in a field or on a low-class berth of a ship, such was his unpressed and unshaven appearance. In short, he was a rumpled mess. On seeing me he leapt to his feet, dark-eyed and wild of gaze, held out a spindly hand and grasped my own with force.

'Savage!' he informed me in a roar. 'Orinoco Savage. Captain – King's Shropshire Light Infantry. Father was an explorer, named me after a river in the Americas. Damned lucky I didn't end up with a sister called Amazon – hah-ha!' He released my crushed hand at last. 'Good of you – very civil. Most grateful.' With that he regained his seat as if some fuse inside him had momentarily been extinguished.

Introductions to the ladies were now in order, while my mother busied herself heating the pot of broth on the fire. The mistress whose shrieks had pierced the night was a Mrs Venetia Merchant. I noted that she had claimed the most comfortable chair beside the fire, close to the hefty black object. I now observed this to be a tin trunk. With her bonnet removed, I saw that Mrs Merchant was a woman in her mid thirties, her hair of an ordinary sort of brown and caught up in some complicated style. Her face was plain and wore a permanent expression of peevish complaint.

'I am distraught!' she announced, offering me a hand so lacking in force it could not have been more different from that of Captain Savage. 'I need to return to London – to my husband, my boys! They will be bereft without me!'

Quite close to her perched a faded, kindly-looking lady called Miss Hedges. 'Oh, my dear,' she comforted her, 'I'm sure we shall be able to make progress in the morning and that we shall all be safely home by tomorrow night. I do feel sure my friend Miss Turner, who is expecting me, will be beside herself with worry. But what can we do except to expect only the best?' Miss Hedges gave me a sweet smile and I decided that she was a safe and gentle person.

I turned at length to the last of the company. Seated on one of the chairs by the table was the young woman, who, without her bonnet, I saw, had dark hair wound in a modest arrangement. She wore a plain grey dress and her eyes were cast shyly towards the floor. With her pale complexion and calm demeanour she looked to me like the painting of a saint, or even the virgin mother of our Lord.

'This young lady is Miss Ellen Gibson,' my mother informed me, since neither Ellen nor anyone else seemed about to introduce her. 'She's maidservant to Mrs Merchant here.'

Ellen Gibson raised her eyes to me for a moment. In those few seconds I saw a long face with well-proportioned lips, neither too thick nor too thin, and the merest hint of pink in her cheeks. But in her brown eyes, deep and lustrous, I read an expression of such misery and desperate appeal that I was quite taken aback.

'G'd evening,' she breathed, before returning her gaze to our brick floor.

'Ellen is a cripple,' Mrs Merchant informed us brusquely. 'She was lucky to find anyone to take her on, but I like to show charity where I can.'

'Er – good evening, Miss Gibson,' I replied, feeling quite shaken. I recalled her limping gait as she crossed the platform. Taking advantage now of her downcast eyes I took in the waves of hair about her forehead, the strong set of her shoulders and the neat way she sat, her feet tucked under the chair. She seemed, I thought, at everyone's mercy, and a heat of tender protective sweetness flamed in me.

This I found most unsettling. I moved to assist my mother, resolving to keep well away from Miss Gibson. I knew that the wiles of women are many and various.

'Now,' my dear mother announced, 'here's soup for everyone.'

She and I fed the company and I took what we could spare to the waiting room, pushing in the pot through the door without entering myself. I did not want to know of their activities with the demon drink. The thought that a man of the cloth considered it fit to partake in them disturbed me more than I could express. But I was further disturbed by the thought of Ellen Gibson, whose quiet form, with its female apparatus of curves, I could not banish from my thoughts. I almost wished I could run her out into the snow for the way that in those seconds of her humiliation she had snagged my foolish heart.

The snow fell silently and I hurried back to our muffled cottage. I heard the murmur of voices as the group made acquaintance with each other. 'Make me pure as this snow in your eyes, Lord,' I was praying as I unlatched the door. 'Banish any thoughts which are not . . .' But I was inside and did not finish.

I positioned myself on a chair the other side of the room from Miss Gibson, beside the strange army captain. In his trumpet voice he was regaling the company with tales of the Indian Mutiny in '57, in which he had played a lively part at Lucknow. It was not until they had all partaken of warm mince pies and the kettle was whistling on the fire that anyone paid attention to the tin trunk, taking up such a portion of space and warmth.

Captain Savage had been eating as if it was his first meal in days. Replete enough now, however, he reached into his breast pocket and brought forth a leather pouch. He drew from it – at first I thought my eyes deceived me – a mouse. It was quite dead and as he grasped it by the tail I heard a small sound from across the room. Only then did I look at Miss Gibson. Her eyes were fixed on the mouse. The desperate look was banished and her face had come alive with interest. My own fascination was divided between the sudden loveliness I saw in her features and the mouse being dangled before us.

'Ugh!' cried Mrs Merchant. 'What on earth are you doing with that disgusting thing! Get it out of here!'

'Ah, no, madam,' Captain Savage cried. 'Do we not all deserve to eat? In here—' he got up and stepped over to the trunk – 'now, I hope, safely enjoying this warm refuge, I have the care of a creature more used to tropical climes.'

'Oh my,' I heard my mother exclaim from beside me. Miss Hedges' nervous expression had become even more uncertain, but she sat politely. I allowed myself another glance at Miss Gibson, at those dark, burning eyes, and looked away again quickly. For a second, before I could curb my wayward thoughts, I had in my mind a picture of her standing before me, those eyes fixed thus passionately on mine . . . Oh, Thomas, I groaned inwardly. Thou art a hopeless sinner.

'What on earth can you mean?' Mrs Venetia Merchant was rapidly removing herself from the best chair, close to the trunk, and backing across the room. 'Ellen,' she ordered, 'exchange places with me.'

I could not tear my eyes away. With reluctance I thought born more out of self-consciousness at her affliction than fear of the contents of the trunk, Ellen Gibson stood up. She limped across the room, her gaze lowered in embarrassment. It seemed to me there was some problem at the level of her hip which cast her walking so. But instead of sitting she stood near the chair to watch.

'This,' Captain Savage announced, tapping the trunk with the toe of one of his boots, while still holding the mouse, 'contains a fine example of the Burmese python. This specimen is on her way to the London Zoological Gardens . . .'

'A *snake*?' Mrs Merchant cried vaporously. 'You can't mean – in there? A giant *reptile* – oh!' She put her hand to her forehead and began to move towards the door. 'Oh, Ellen – take me away from here!'

Ellen Gibson did not move. She stood with her eyes shining, staring at the trunk. Mrs Merchant, realizing the futility of any escape she might make, returned further impassioned.

'Get that thing *out* of here,' she ordered.

'No, no, madam – be calm.' Captain Savage reached

for a small latch in the side of the trunk and popped the mouse inside before shutting it again. This action and the graceful fall of Ellen Gibson's grey dress occupied my sight, the one inextricable from the other as she was standing so near. 'You're all quite safe. The creature is locked in and is most likely sleeping, recovering from the ordeal of such terrible cold. Do, please, take your seat again.'

'My goodness,' Miss Hedges was exclaiming, among the general chatter. 'I've never seen any such thing. I assume it can't get out?'

'One of God's creatures, I suppose,' my mother soothed her. I admired her calm amid all this disturbance. 'Let's all make ourselves comfortable again while I mash the tea, shall we?'

It was several hours before a drowsiness came over the company. Mrs Merchant, regretting having surrendered her prize chair, ordered her maid to restore it to her and help her move it further away from the trunk, at which she glanced frequently with a wary frown. Every few moments she dispatched orders to Miss Gibson – 'A footstool, Ellen!' 'Help me to sit comfortably, girl!' 'Fetch the cologne from my reticule!' Each time Ellen Gibson stood, moving with painful awkwardness to obey her commands, my wayward eyes could not but follow, drinking in each movement and line of her. While she was not pretty exactly, the shape of her had entirely bewitched me. The emotions condensed into those brown, downcast eyes, of which I had had only glimpses, tore at me as if they were my own. What intense feeling was concealed within that breast, which had telegraphed unwittingly from her eyes, so dark and full of yearning? I found myself longing to let this young woman lean her head upon my shoulder, to comfort her with words assuring her that her torment was at an end. And yet how I wanted to avoid her, for her to leave my sight so that my usual peace might be restored.

My dear mother made sure that the company were as comfortable as could be. The captain, meanwhile, recounted story after story about exploits among the snow leopards of the Himalayas, pig-sticking forays from the cantonments of northern India and his expeditions into the jungles of Burma. While on any other night I should have been entranced by such novelty, tonight I was in a fever. I longed for quiet, for every eye except my own two to close so that I might safely watch Ellen Gibson. She, absorbed at first in these exotic tales, at last bent gracefully forward, her head resting on her arms on the table.

At last, in various positions of repose, they all lapsed into silence. But I was far from sleep. From my seat I could see the rosy incline of her cheek, a curl of hair resting soft over her ear, and see the faint movement of her breathing in the grey curve of her back. She was the most beautiful thing I had ever seen. I promised the Lord that after tonight I should never more cast a glance towards any female, never again imagine the pale mounds and curvature that must lie under her simple attire. But tonight, sinner as I was, I was lost to it. My imagination was far hotter than the fire, which, once some hours had passed, I had the presence of mind to notice was dying in the grate.

'Where are you going?'

It was a whisper behind me as I unlatched the door. She was on her feet, reaching for her cloak. Shadows made hollow patches on her face and neck.

'For wood,' I replied. My heart was a piston in my chest. We were, in essence, alone, for the others were absent in sleep.

'I'll come with you,' she said. There was a hesitation in her voice, but who was I to discourage her?

'The snow's let up,' I said as we stepped out: I closing the door, she covering her hair with her hood. A few flakes were still dropping, like the last scraps from a wastepaper basket. I had doused the station lights hours ago, but even in the darkness, all about us glowed white. Whatever revels had taken place in the waiting room had by now died out.

All was quiet, even our footsteps as she limped beside me. She told me she had contracted tuberculosis in her hip as a child. Something of her shape, of the awkward, lurching way she walked, seemed somehow familiar and right to me, as if I had known her before, or had always been waiting to know her. I saw no deficit in her walk, only grace, and I said so. She was silent after, and I wondered if I had spoken wrongly.

'Will they get us out tomorrow?' she said, in her soft country accent, adding, 'or p'raps it's today now?'

'Oh yes,' I said, enjoying my knowledge. We walked around to the back to our wood store. 'They'll send up an engine with a snowplough to clear the line from ———. You'll be on your way soon. But still—' in my nerves I chattered on – 'if you hadn't been waylaid here, you'd never have seen the captain, and that snake – or its container, at least.'

Ellen Gibson, to my astonishment, gave a full-throated laugh. 'You don't really believe there's a snake in there, do you?'

I gaped at her. 'Yes! Well . . . *Yes!* Why else would he say . . . ? And the mouse . . . !'

Her face, all smiles, was a wonder to me. Her dark eyes showed clear in that pale face framed by her hood, and a dimple appeared as a cheery dot to the left of her mouth.

'Oh, Thomas,' she said, merry now. 'You don't want to believe everything people tell you! I'd be willing to bet there's just a pile of old rugs in there. That fellow's touched in the upper storey, if you ask me. Gracious me – how old are you? You're innocent as a lamb!'

But it was spoken kindly. I swallowed, with a sudden longing to be less innocent. 'I'm twenty-seven,' I said.

'Well, I'm nineteen, but I seem to have seen more of the world than you.' She was standing close to me, by the wood store. I tried to repossess myself, reaching for my sack to fill with branches.

'You must see a good deal more of life, living in London,' I said.

'I hate London. And I hate *her*, Mrs Merchant.' Her voice had lowered suddenly, to a quiet intensity. 'I'm glad we're stuck here. We don't have to go back to London, to her pompous husband she hardly sees and her sons who scarcely know who she is. Miss Ann their nanny's a mother to them, not her.'

I had straightened up and was listening. It was dark and cold, but never had I felt warmer or more entranced. I drank in the sight of her and loved the country curves of her speech, not unlike mine.

'D'you know, Thomas,' this wonder of a person continued, 'I grew up in the orphanage – in Middlesex.

Before I went into service I thought families were all a magical thing and that rich people knew how to live. But they don't, not this lot, anyway. They don't know the first thing about . . . About being *alive.*'

She half saw my face in the dark, which must have held an astonished expression. 'I shouldn't be talking like this, I know – but I've no one, *ever*, to say anything to.'

I was rooted to the spot, arms full of wood. And by the Lord, had they not been I can't say what I might have done. I knew not what to reply. I was so hopeless, like a rusty machine that has made no progress in years. All I could think of was, 'Oh – that doesn't sound very nice.'

Ellen looked at me from inside the hood. A flake of snow fell on her nose and she wiped it off.

'You're a funny one,' she observed.

'I s'pose I am,' I admitted. 'I've been shut away down here a long while.'

'That's not a bad thing,' she said. 'Life's no better in the city.'

I stood staring foolishly at her. I could have stood there the rest of the night, just with her in my view. She had blocked out everything else.

'You'd better put that firewood down,' she said. As we turned, she added, 'I like talking to you.' And my heart swelled until I thought it would burst. I did put the firewood down, threw it down right beside me, and I took Ellen Gibson in my arms. Her chest met mine, her eyes sweet and eager, just as were her tender lips. We stood out in the glow of the snow and under the moon. For a long time we were heedless of the cold, wrapped in each other, in the wonder of our first kisses. I had never known life could be so thrilling and yet so gentle, or that joy could trumpet so loud within me while the night was yet so silent and still.

When we did creep inside, all was quiet, except for a few snores. As I went to rekindle the fire I eyed the trunk, wondering how I had so readily believed there was a giant snake inside when I had so little proof. And how, despite my doubting name, I had so readily believed so many things I had been told by people of supposed authority.

Christmas Eve dawned glittering bright. Sunshine across the woods and white fields raised everyone to jubilation. The men emerged from the waiting room, all hearty except for the reverend, Cecil Walmsley, whose face looked decidedly green against the surrounding white. The barrel was rolled out, empty of its contents.

My mother cut bread for our breakfast, though I could scarcely eat. We men took turns with shovels to clear the tracks. I worked like a man in a fever after a night of no sleep and with my body in a new, splendid state of exaltation. Oh, the power and joy of woman! The miracle of love! My mind was taken up completely by the person of Ellen Gibson, the miraculous feel and scent of her, by the swell of her bosom which only a short time ago had been pressed to my thundering chest.

'You're nice, you are, Thomas Lee,' were the simple words she said after our lips parted and she, enclosed by my arms, looked up at me. But those words were enough to set the whole course of my life. Oh, I had become a man, in every wish and need. I experienced the power of a woman's closeness, the gift of Christmas a thousandfold. I was baptized in love – in life!

I could not think of the departure, the moment when the engine would get up steam and pull the company away, those remaining miles to ———, then another, onward, to the great city of London, so distant and unknown to me. Such was my state that I was, like my station, snowed into an eternal present where there was no forward movement, yet all was possible. I was in love. I was now – that was all.

Mother supplied us with hot tea to fuel our labours. By eleven we menfolk, shovelling on the track, saw a plume of smoke rise from beyond the trees. The sound of the train grew and a cry rose. We stood on the platform and cheered – even the sour Mrs Merchant – as the engine appeared, a metal wedge plough on the front, forcing the snow aside. Ellen stood quiet, and I could not at that moment know her thoughts.

'The Lord be praised!' cheered Cecil Walmsley groggily.

'London by tonight!' bawled Captain Savage. 'My precious creature shall be delivered. I must carry her aboard!'

My eyes met Ellen's. Did we believe? I knew I should never ask.

'Come along, girl,' Venetia Merchant commanded. 'Fetch our things! We shall be going.'

At midday, the engine began to move. Percy, Bob and Ernie fell to their tasks. Percy winked at me from the footplate. 'Had a good night, then, have you, lad?' To my deep annoyance my face flamed with blushes.

The train puffed and shrieked, then creaked into movement. They were going – would be gone! My heart leapt and thudded. The train containing these strangely met companions was leaving; one of them, a Mrs Venetia Merchant, with a face like a study in rage itself at the last-minute defection of her maid.

We waved the train goodbye. Ellen's hand was clasped in mine, warm and strong, for she is a powerful, loving woman, who over the years birthed our five children with an air of being born to it. She has been a helpmeet at all times, to myself and my mother. There would be talk of reading the banns, of marriage and all the practicalities of a shared life to come. But at this moment, as the train faded to a dark smudge between the banks of snow, I pulled her to me, an arm around her waist. My Ellen. My love.

A Railway Christmas

ANNIE MURRAY

*One of my favourite Christmas memories is of a
very different sort of Christmas that was spent far
away from home . . .*

*We were called 'Bogiewallahs' – travellers in a
converted Indian railway carriage or 'Bogie'.*

*This Bogie was organized by Butterfields
Railway Tours, run by a dauntless Yorkshireman
called Ashley Butterfield. Over the Christmas of
1979, Ashley was to have time off. I worked as an
assistant to a deputy leader for a five-week tour,
living in 'the Bogie', as it was fondly known. By
arrangement with Indian Railways the Bogie was
coupled to trains following a route round India
and had room for about thirty passengers.*

*The only thing that distinguished it from all
the other umber-coloured railway carriages was
a small poster on the side. One common feature
of life lived on the railway was going along to the
loos and returning to find that the engines in the
yard – many still steam in those days – had
been shunting (again). You had to search, dodging*

across the shunting-yard tracks, to find out where the Bogie had got to this time!

Every aspect of life was an adventure. We cooked in a tiny kitchen in the middle of the carriage, on four fire buckets set into a clay surround on the floor. As well as the business of lighting the coals in the buckets (sometimes hanging out of the door of a moving train to get a breeze to them), the huge cooking pans had no handles but were lifted by a lip at the edge. Shifting these about on a moving train was dangerous, to say the least – but is what cooks have been doing on Indian trains for years, just as all food was prepared while squatting on the floor.

We spent Christmas Day in Cochin in Kerala. Cochin is a port, a place of spice warehouses, famous for its beautiful fishing nets hanging like graceful moths from bamboos all along the seafront. Lunchtime was for rest, plenty of chat and jokes and curry. We celebrated with the passengers at a restaurant in the town. But on Christmas night we were scheduled to move on north, travelling overnight.

It was a very hot evening and all of us were warmed inwardly by a good spicy meal. The food schedule for the tour had to be followed, however: supper was to be pea and ham soup. Obediently we filled the fire buckets from the coal bunker in the kitchen and set to on the soup. As we cooked, the train eased into motion and we were soon thrumming along through the suburbs. What with the heat outside and the fires inside, the cutlery in the kitchen was soon too hot to touch! Sweat poured off us. The passengers peeped in sympathetically.

'We don't really need soup,' they said. 'We had such a good lunch.'

'Too late!' we said with moist cheeriness.

At last the unnecessary meal was over and done with, and with the carriage doors open, most of us relaxed, chatting, on the floor. We breathed in the soft night air as our engine pulled us onwards into Boxing Day and to a new destination. No presents, no tree or streamers – but it was a wonderful Christmas.

You'll Never Know Just How Much I Love You

Pam Weaver

Anita . . . Anita . . . he couldn't stop saying her name. It wasn't on his lips, he didn't dare say it out loud, but it was in his head all the time. Anita. She was like a film star. She was better than a film star, better than Betty Grable, lovelier than Carole Lombard, and she had prettier hair than Veronica Lake.

With a sigh, John glanced up at the clock. Three forty-six. It seemed like an age since he'd last looked, but the hands stubbornly refused to move. Their last customer had come in at around two o'clock and that was only to bring in a card for his employer, Mrs Stephens. It was obvious that no one else was going to come into the post office now and even if they did, since it was Christmas Eve, they hadn't got a hope of getting a card or a letter delivered by the next day. In fact, even though there was a war on, there would be no post for the next two days.

He was bored and frustrated but Mrs Stephens hadn't let him remain idle. He'd cleaned the windows and updated the meagre displays. He'd replaced the outdated forms with new government issues. He'd tidied the stationery cupboard and filled up the coal scuttle to keep the pot-bellied stove going. The weather outside was deteriorating all the time. There was no sign of snow but the wind had got up and it was raining. He wished he could leave before it got any worse, but as Mrs Stephens reminded him, the post office hours were 9.00 to 5.30 and he was honour-bound to stay. 'As our only telegram boy,' she'd said firmly, 'you have a responsibility, dear.'

The post office at Goring-by-Sea was an imposing building with a 1930s mock-Georgian front, and the entrance was up a series of steps. The telephone exchange was next door and the sorting office was at the back. They'd closed at noon, lucky devils. John sighed again. They must be the only place in Worthing still open for business, he thought bitterly.

At seventeen, he'd been lucky to get this job with the GPO. 'A job for life,' his mother had told him, but John wasn't so sure he wanted that. It was 1943 and the war was still going strong, even though they'd said it would all be over by that first Christmas. The whole country was war-weary. As soon as he was old enough, John planned to join up and finish the job his father had started. He was destined for better things than being a general dogsbody and telegram boy for the GPO. He would send old Hitler and his lot packing, and when he came back home a hero he would marry Anita Barton.

Uncle Jack said that he was too young to know about such things as love and marriage, but whenever he thought of Anita he had a funny feeling in the pit of his stomach, and every time he saw her his heart would race. She would smile at him, but until he had proved himself he was afraid to tell her how he felt. Then his sister, Margie, had told him Anita and her best friend were both stepping out with some Canadians. That drove him to despair. What chance did he have against some chap with plenty of money and a pretty uniform?

'You look miles away,' said Mrs Stephens, bringing him back to the here and now. 'Are you doing anything special for Christmas?'

'Not really,' said John, 'just me, Mum and my sister.'

'That's nice,' said Mrs Stephens, glancing up. She had been checking the stamps in the big book. 'Let's have a cup of tea, shall we?'

A minute later he heard her in the kitchen pouring water into the tin kettle.

As Mrs Stephens brought in two cups of tea and put

them on the counter, the telegraph machine burst into life. Putting her glasses back on, Mrs Stephens sat at the desk as the tape came through.

John picked up his cup and sipped the dark, scalding liquid. Judging by the way the rain was coming down, he was in for a wet ride on his bicycle to deliver the message. He hoped it wasn't too far.

Mrs Stephens busied herself sticking the taped message onto the buff-coloured form. 'You'd better get ready, John,' she said dully. 'This has to go straight away.'

He didn't need her to tell him what sort of message it was. Her expression told him it wasn't good news. What a bugger . . . giving someone bad news on Christmas Eve. He pulled on his coat quickly, muffling his mouth with his scarf. The wind whistled around the corner of the building. He'd have a job keeping his cap on in this weather.

'Go carefully,' said Mrs Stephens, seeing him to the door. 'I'll pop in to your mother on the way home and tell her where you are. When you've delivered it, go straight home. Have a nice Christmas, dear.'

'You too, Mrs Stephens,' he said. 'See you on Wednesday.'

She handed him the telegram.

'Where to?'

'Keeper's Cottage in Titnore Lane,' she said. 'It's for Mrs Barton.'

John's heart sank. That was Anita's place. Something dreadful must have happened to her brother.

Anita was putting the finishing touches to the Christmas cake while her mother told her little brother and sister a bedtime story upstairs. This was her first attempt to do the cake on her own, and she was proud of her achievement. Everyone was determined to have a better Christmas than last year, although it was still impossible to make the festivities as exciting as they had been before her father's death from TB in 1939. And that hadn't been the end of their troubles. Her brother Paul was called up as soon as the war started, and shortly after they'd waved him goodbye, he was posted missing in action. Anita's mother had aged overnight.

Balancing a tired-looking and chipped Father Christmas in the middle of the cake, she pushed a tendril of russet-coloured hair away from her eyes and stepped back to admire her handiwork. The cake was made with reconstituted eggs, and covered with mock marzipan. The recipe had said sixteen ounces of dried fruit but she had only managed to get hold of three-quarters of a pound. Luckily the twins were too young to remember the cakes they'd baked before the war, so she was sure they'd love it.

Putting the cake in the pantry, Anita wiped the drop-down pastry board on the kitchen cupboard and closed it up. She wanted to be helpful, but there was another reason for her activity. She was missing Freda dreadfully and this would be her first Christmas without her. She and her best friend had been inseparable. They'd sat next to each other at school, and enjoyed going to the pictures, swimming off the jetty at Goring and biking out in the country. They were both fifteen when the war came, and when they left school they both became typists. Anita went to work for the police while Freda took a temporary job in Ferring. Both girls planned to join the WAAFs as soon as they were old enough. They'd met up regularly at dances, but then Freda began to date someone. As a result, they'd seen less and less of each other and it was some time before Anita found out what had happened to Freda. She shook away the memory and decided to put out the Christmas fare.

She and the twins had spent the afternoon making the front room look quite festive. Hung with newspaper paper chains, it was decorated with holly and ivy from the woods, and they'd put Epsom salts onto the fir cones. Spread thickly enough, it dried to look like snow. Anita put a plate of cobnuts, collected in September and left to ripen, next to her mother's armchair, and the home-made sweets she'd made, from the extra ration of sugar the government had allowed them for the holiday, in the centre of the table. The big treat they had lined up for tomorrow was some cream, standing in a jug on the floor of the pantry to keep cool. They would have it with the pudding.

In the run-up to Christmas, Anita had made her little sister, Christine, a nurse's uniform and her mother had managed to buy a toy Spitfire plane for Christopher. It wasn't much, but the country was fighting for its life and the children understood that their mother and big sister were doing the best they could. As for her mother's present, Anita had saved money from her wage packet to buy wool and a pattern and had spent every moment she could knitting a jumper. It had been a bit of a rush towards the end and she'd had to use some old buttons for the opening at the back, but she'd finally finished it on 21st December. Safe in the knowledge that her mother didn't know anything about it, she'd wrapped the jumper in Christmas paper lovingly taken off and ironed from the year before and the year before that.

Doris came back downstairs. 'Phew,' she smiled, 'that was a bit of a marathon. They both wanted long stories. I let them have one each tonight . . . well, it's Christmas.'

'Sit down, Mum. I'll make you a cup of tea.'

'No,' said Doris. 'Tell you what. You've been so helpful and the room looks lovely. Let's start our Christmas a bit early. Get two glasses, Nita, and we'll have some of my home-made ginger wine.'

Anita reached into the cupboard and got down two of the imitation crystal glasses inherited from Grandma and opened the bottle. She poured the rich dark wine into the glasses and sat opposite her mother. 'Here's to our Paul and to absent friends,' said Doris, raising her glass. 'God bless them and give us all a happy Christmas.'

'And here's to the end of the war.' Anita raised her glass and sipped. The ginger burned her throat, but it wasn't an unpleasant feeling.

'So when are you back on duty?' her mother asked as they relaxed.

'Not until Wednesday,' Anita smiled. 'That's the one advantage of having Christmas day on a Saturday.' She loved her job at Worthing police station, where she worked behind the desk. She spent most of her day typing and making tea, and even though it wasn't a reserved occupation, she felt as if she were doing her bit for the country. Her mother was in a good mood so she took the plunge. 'Mum, there's a policeman's ball on New Year's Eve. Can I go? It's in the Assembly Rooms.'

'I don't see why not,' said her mother. 'You'll be with Freda, won't you?'

And without thinking Anita blurted out, 'Well, she wouldn't be able to go now, would she?'

Doris looked startled. 'What on earth do you mean?'

Anita blushed a deep crimson. 'Oh, Mum, I shouldn't

have said that. You won't tell anyone, will you?'

Doris sat up. 'What are you talking about?'

'Freda is in trouble.'

'What sort of trouble . . .' The words died on her lips as the penny dropped. 'You mean . . . ?'

'She's having a baby,' Anita nodded. 'She's gone to stay with her aunty in Bristol. I was supposed to keep it secret. Oh, Mum, don't say anything, please.'

'Of course not,' said Doris. 'Was it that singer in the band?'

Anita nodded.

Her mother sighed. 'Poor, silly girl.'

The driver was hunched over the steering wheel. The storm had come quickly, and now that it was dark, visibility was practically nil. There were no street lights, and because of the blackout he couldn't see any house lights either. Everywhere was so damned dark. The shaded headlights on the front of the truck were no better than candles. The rain was coming down like knives and the wind was so gusty that every now and then he struggled to keep the vehicle on the road. Stuffed full of fish paste sandwiches and English tea, his passengers dozed in the back of the truck. In the interests of fostering good relations with the locals, they had just finished performing an afternoon tea dance at some village hall way out in the sticks. Surprisingly, the place had been packed and the band, although hastily put together, sounded quite good. As usual, Woody, the singer, had had every female heart from sixteen to sixty racing.

When he'd signed up for C Company Royal 22nd Regiment in his home town of Alberta, Clarence had thought he'd be fighting in Europe. He hadn't banked on being posted to a small village called Goring-by-Sea on the outskirts of Worthing, but it wasn't so bad. In between laying barbed wire on the beaches and doing manoeuvres in the woods, the company kept the locals amused in more ways than one. There was talk of an Allied offensive, but he had a feeling it would be next year before that got under way. The war wasn't going well.

A deer suddenly sprang across the road. Clarence slammed on the brakes almost immediately, but still came within a whisker of hitting the animal. The deer leapt through a gap in the hedge on the opposite side of the road and was quickly followed by another and then another.

As he'd braked he heard a couple of thumps in the back of the truck as his passengers fell off the wooden seat. Seconds later, a sleepy voice said, 'Hey. What are you doing, man?'

'Wildlife on the move,' said Clarence, blowing out his cheeks with relief.

Woody stuck his head through the tarpaulin curtain which divided the back of the truck from the cab and yawned. 'How much further?'

'Four miles,' Clarence shrugged, 'maybe five.'

Just ahead of him, Clarence could dimly make out the shape of a man with some sort of sack on his back, coming out of the woods.

'Poacher,' Clarence muttered.

The guy glanced at the truck and began to run. At the same time a bicycle was coming up the lane towards them. The rider had his head bowed over the handlebars as he struggled to make headway in the wind and driving rain.

'Poor sod,' Clarence said. 'This is no night to be bike riding.'

He shifted the gear and prepared to move off but as he put his foot on the accelerator, something moved at the corner of his eye. 'Holy shit!' He had hardly got the words out of his mouth before a huge tree hit the road in front of them, earth from its roots peppering the windscreen.

A split second later, Clarence was out of the cab. The only sounds were the howl of the wind and the hiss of hot water escaping from the radiator fractured by a branch as the tree fell. The other guys clambered out of the back of the truck.

Clarence peered into the gloom. 'Hey buddy. You OK?'

'Who are you yelling at?' Woody asked.

'There was a guy with a sack right in front of the tree, and some other guy on a bike,' said Clarence. There was no sign of either of them now and Clarence felt sick. If the men were under the trunk they'd be the width of a dollar bill. To his immense relief, the cyclist stood up and brushed himself down. Clarence could see now that he was just a kid, maybe sixteen or seventeen.

'You all right, kid?'

John nodded. 'It came down right in front of me,' he said with an unmistakable tremor in his voice. 'If it had been a second later, I'd have been killed.'

'You and me both,' said Clarence sagely.

All at once, the man with the sack appeared, and before John could gather his wits, the man had grabbed his bike. John was pushed to the ground, but he wasn't going to let the bike go that easily. 'Oi!' He made a grab at the man's leg as he turned the bike around. 'Get off it.'

They wrestled for a second or two before the man managed to shake him off. By now John was on his feet, but he wasn't quite quick enough. The man had already mounted the bike. John made a last grab for him and pulled open the sack on the man's back. A chicken's head appeared. John wasn't sure which of them was the more startled, the chicken or himself, but the bird managed to make a noisy dash for freedom as the bicycle thief took the opportunity to ride off.

John put his hands on his head as he watched the bike disappearing into the gloom. The chicken had sauntered towards the woods, where it began to scratch the earth for food. Whipping off his coat, John threw it over the bird before it could make another getaway.

By now the men from the truck had climbed over the fallen trunk and were standing beside him. 'Can you believe the nerve of that guy?' Clarence asked.

John knew as soon as Clarence opened his mouth that they were Canadian soldiers. Miserably, he picked up his coat and the chicken. He was in big trouble. That bike was GPO property.

'I'm getting wet and it's damned cold,' Woody said. 'Where the hell are we?'

'Titnore Lane,' said John. His shirt was soaked and he could feel the rain trickling down his back. He remembered the telegram in his top pocket and hoped it wasn't damaged. The chicken clucked miserably and John shivered and sneezed.

Clarence laid his hand on the tree trunk. 'It's going to take quite a few men to move this thing off the road,' he said. 'Any houses around here?'

'Keeper's Cottage,' said John. 'I was on my way there myself. It's not far.'

'Do they have a telephone?' asked Woody.

John shook his head. 'You'd have to go to the station for that.' He pointed in the direction from which he'd come. 'It's the other side of the crossroads. You can't miss it.'

After a brief conversation, the men decided to walk there for help. Clarence looked anxiously at John. 'How far is this Keeper's Cottage?'

'About a hundred yards,' said John, sneezing again.

'We gotta get you outta this rain,' said Clarence.

So the men parted, four of them heading towards the station with their instruments while Clarence and Woody let John, with the chicken under his arm, lead the way to Keeper's Cottage.

The knock on the door came as a surprise. Being separated from the rest of the village by several acres of farmland, Anita and her mother didn't get many visitors.

'Excuse me, Ma'am,' Clarence began as the door opened, 'we could do with some help.'

'Come in, come in,' cried Doris.

Woody pushed his way inside and Anita caught her breath. She recognized him at once. What was he doing here? She heard someone stumble by the door and turned. 'Johnny!' She grabbed his arm. 'You're soaked to the skin.'

The chicken under his arm clucked helplessly.

'We caught someone trying to steal one of your hens,' said John hoarsely.

'We'd better put it back with the others,' said Anita, grabbing her coat from the nail on the door and reaching for her wellingtons.

'I hope he hasn't let them all out,' Doris wailed as they left. 'They're good layers.'

The chickens were roosting in the henhouse and a quick count revealed that all were present and correct. 'It's not ours,' said Anita, relieved. 'He must have pinched it from the farm.'

'We can't put it in with the others,' said John. 'Strange chicken in the coop: the others will peck it to death. Have you got anywhere else it could go?'

In the end, they put it under the covered run Doris used to rear her pullets. John weighted the run down with some logs so that any passing fox couldn't tip it up, and Anita pulled a piece of tarpaulin over one end to give the chicken some shelter. 'That'll have to do for tonight,' she said. 'We'll take it back in the morning.'

Back in the house, Clarence was helping Doris in the kitchen where she was making them tea. Woody was sprawled across the armchair, his back against one arm and his feet dangling over the side of the other. He had made short work of Anita's home-made sweets and was busy cracking nuts. Anita glared at him angrily.

'What?' he challenged. 'I'm hungry.'

She didn't say anything. She couldn't. She knew she wouldn't be civil.

'Oh, my dear,' said Doris, looking at John. 'You're like a drowned rat.'

Anita took John to the scullery and gave him hot water, soap and towels. Doris found some of Paul's things, some underwear and a jumper. John protested loudly that he couldn't possibly wear them, but they took his wet things to dry in front of the fire while he got cleaned up, so he had no choice. It was awful putting Paul's things on. What would they say when he gave them the telegram? Anita would hate him forever.

When he came back, Clarence was sitting at the table. Anita and Doris were upstairs settling the twins down.

'Wanna nut?' said Woody, his mouth full of bits. 'They're quite nice.'

Clarence looked up. 'Don't eat them all.'

'Why not?' laughed Woody. 'It's Christmas.'

'And that's probably all they have,' John remarked sourly.

'They've got plenty more stashed away somewhere,' Woody insisted. 'My mom kept everything hidden until Christmas Day.'

Anita had entered the room. She didn't say anything but John's heart sank as he saw Woody flashing her a disarming smile. What chance did he have against someone like him? He was handsome, manly and so sure of himself. 'Hope you don't mind,' Woody said, indicating the almost empty bowl of nuts, 'but we ain't had no dinner.'

Anita sat down, still staring at him. 'I could make you a sandwich.'

'God, no. No more sandwiches,' said Woody. 'Been eating the damned things all afternoon.'

'We've been to a tea dance,' said Clarence by way of explanation.

'I know you,' said Woody, looking at Anita. 'You were at the Assembly Rooms with that girl with the curly hair. What was she called?' Woody clicked his fingers as he tried to remember her name.

'Freda,' said Anita.

'Yeah, that's right. Whatever happened to her? She was a nice kid.'

Doris came into the room. 'Let's hope they stay settled now. I'm worn out.'

'We oughta get going,' said Clarence quickly. 'Thanks for the tea, Ma'am.'

'Don't rush away on my account,' said Doris. 'Wait until the rain eases off a bit. Nita, get some of your lovely Christmas cake.'

Woody gave John an 'I told you so' look and threw the nutcrackers on top of the empty shells. Anita got the cake and cut everyone a slice.

John smiled as she gave him a plate. 'This looks really good.'

Woody held his plate up to the light. 'Is this supposed to be a fruit cake?'

Anita bristled with anger.

'It's hard to get hold of fruit,' said Doris quickly. 'Everything is rationed.'

'You never did tell me about Freda,' said Woody, his mouth full of cake. 'We had some good times.'

'And you ruined her life,' said Anita coldly.

John choked on his cake and Woody sat up straight. 'Now wait a minute . . .'

'No, you wait a minute,' said Anita coldly. 'You told her you would get married.'

'Nita,' said Doris. 'Woody is our guest.'

'He may be yours, Mum,' Anita countered, 'but he's certainly not mine.'

John held his breath. She was magnificent.

'I think . . .' Clarence began awkwardly.

'Listen, honey,' Woody snapped, 'it was just a bit of fun. It don't mean a thing.'

'It did to Freda.'

Woody shrugged. 'How was I to know she was taking it serious?'

'Well, she did,' said Anita. 'You're a disgrace to your uniform.'

Woody leapt to his feet and would have pushed his

face into Anita's had not John jumped between them. Clarence was on his feet as well.

'Oh, please,' cried Doris, throwing her hands into the air. 'Stop it, all of you. Don't do this. It's Christmas Eve.'

'You know how it is,' said Woody sitting down. 'A few drinks, some nice dance music and a little moonlight . . . it must have gone to her head.'

'And now she's having your baby.'

The words hung in the room like icicles waiting to fall. Looking at the anguish on Anita's face, all John wanted to do was hold her. Poor Freda. He'd had no idea.

Woody gasped. 'A baby!'

'You could still put it right,' said Anita jumping up and going to the mantelpiece. She took down a letter. 'I've got her address here. You could write to her. Tell her you'll marry her and then she won't have to give the baby up.'

Clarence groaned and put his head in his hands.

Woody's lip curled. 'How do you know it's mine?' John made a disgusted sound and Woody spun round. 'It's a reasonable question. The girl was easy.'

And that's when John punched him.

Woody staggered but he didn't return the punch. He held his nose. 'What are you, stupid or somethin'? That hurt.'

Clarence positioned himself between them. 'I'm

sorry, Ma'am,' he said to Doris. 'I think we'd better go.'

'I think you had,' said Doris haughtily.

Woody took his hand away from his face. 'Look at me. I'm bleeding,' he whimpered. 'Oh God, has he spoiled my face? Get me a mirror. What does it look like?'

Anita had been scribbling something on a piece of paper. 'Here,' she said as Clarence and Woody made for the door. 'This is Freda's address. You can write to her and tell her . . .'

Clarence shook his head. 'I'm sorry, Miss,' he said. 'He can't. Woody has a wife and two kids back home.'

The door closed and the room fell silent. John was flexing his sore fist. Anita laid her head on his shoulder and wept tears of frustration. John didn't know what to say but as he gently held her he loved her even more. His hand hurt like hell, but he would have clocked a dozen Canadians for a moment like this.

'Thank you,' Anita whispered as she moved away. 'You were wonderful.'

Doris tipped the empty nutshells onto the fire. Anita wiped her eyes and put what was left of the Christmas cake into the tin. John sat at the table staring blankly ahead. It had been wonderful holding Anita in his arms, but what was she going to think of him when he gave them the telegram?

'You can sleep down here, John,' said Doris. 'Go back in the morning when it's light.'

'My things . . .' John began.

'They're still very wet,' said Doris. 'No, you stay here, dear. They'll be dry in the morning.'

He slept badly, his fitful dozing permeated with night-mares about telling Anita and her mother that Paul was dead. Every time he woke up, he knew he couldn't put it off much longer.

The twins bounded downstairs early to open their presents and Anita followed. 'Happy Christmas, John,' she said shyly.

He was relieved that Anita seemed to have recovered from her disappointment of last night. She was so beau-tiful, even in a threadbare dressing gown and slippers. 'Happy Christmas,' he said, wishing the ground would open up and swallow him and the telegram.

Doris made some tea and they had a boiled egg for breakfast. For a man used to bread and dripping, it was a rare treat. As they chatted, he tried to tell them several times but couldn't bring himself to spoil everything.

As the twins played with their new toys, Clarence came back. He had come alone, carrying a large box. 'A gift from C Company Royal 22nd Regiment,' he said, but they all knew it was his way of apologizing for Woody's behaviour. Inside they found things they could only dream of: among them a tinned fruit cake, biscuits, a tin of salmon, ham and a seven-pound tin of strawberry jam. Best of all, he gave Christopher and Christine some Neilson's Chocolate Rosebuds.

'What a wonderful gift,' cried Doris, 'but it's not right to enjoy this all by ourselves. Clarence, please, you must join us tomorrow afternoon, and John, you must invite your mum and your sister over.'

'Why, thank you, Ma'am,' Clarence nodded.

'You're a good man,' said Doris, patting his arm. 'How providential that you came.'

Clarence grinned. 'You have young John to thank for that.'

'Yes, I was wondering about that,' said Anita, turning to John. 'What were you doing here, Johnny? This is nowhere near your place.'

John felt his face flame. He looked helplessly at Anita. This would be the last time she'd ever speak to him.

'I brought a telegram,' he said faintly.

'A telegram?' Doris panicked. 'Oh, dear Lord. Is it Paul?'

'I don't know,' said John. 'I never read it. It's still in my pocket.'

'Then get it,' she cried.

John found the telegram in his jacket, still hanging over the clothes horse. He held it out to Anita's mother.

'You read it,' she said.

John tore it open.

'*Regret to inform you . . .*' he began. Mrs Barton screamed and almost fainted. Clarence grabbed her and sat her down. Anita snatched the telegram from John's hand. John turned away. All he could hear was Mrs Barton's sobbing.

'Wait a minute, Mum,' cried Anita. '*Regret to inform you, Paul Barton is POW in Germany.*' She smiled eagerly at her mother. 'Don't you see, Mum? He may be a prisoner but he's alive. Paul is alive!'

The next minute Clarence and Doris were laughing and whooping around the kitchen with the twins. Anita gave John a hug. 'Thank you, Johnny. You've given us the best Christmas present ever.'

Their eyes met, and as her lips responded to his kiss, his racing heart told him it was the first of many, many more to come.

My Favourite Christmas Memory

PAM WEAVER

Having worked with children for a large chunk of my life, I have some wonderful Christmas memories, but my favourite has to come from the time when I worked in a private day nursery. The children were all under five and we were doing the nativity play. We had arranged to do the play in the morning when the children would be at their brightest and best, but the owner, who only appeared in the nursery every now and then, wasn't very keen. Apparently mornings didn't suit her terribly well, so for that reason alone we had to change it to the afternoon.

The mothers were invited, as were the local press. It was a bit hectic getting everything done after lunch and some of the children were tired after their long morning, but we managed to make it fun for them. As the children gathered in the corridor in costume, ready to walk into the classroom, to our horror the owner of the nursery began to stuff a big sweet into every child's mouth.

Because the children were too young to follow

a script, we had decided to create a tableau while the narrator (a member of staff) told the story. We had an inkling of trouble ahead when the Angel Gabriel and one of the Wise Men began shoving each other in the corridor in a quest to get a better sweet. One of them ended up in tears, but we sorted out the problem and were confident that the feud had been settled. Despite a few chocolatey faces and a couple of yawning angels, the tableau began to look amazing. The photographer clicked away, but then, keen to get to another nativity play at the local primary school, scooted off. The owner left with him.

This was in the days before mobile phone cameras, which was probably just as well, because when the Angel Gabriel realized that everyone was distracted by people leaving and that he was standing immediately above the Wise Man, he seized a golden opportunity to take his revenge. It was left to me to dive into the fray and part two very angry little boys, but thankfully with a little rearranging of their positions they settled down.

When I stepped back, I could see some of the mothers giggling and realized that a drowsy angel had lain down beside the baby in the manger and gone to sleep with her thumb in her mouth. She looked so sweet that it seemed better to leave her there. Surely nothing else could go wrong . . .

We sang some Christmassy songs and the children were wonderful. Everything was going perfectly until there was a loud clatter on the wooden floor followed by a heart-rending wail from the child playing Mary: 'Jesus's arm has fallen off!'

Nothing could be done, because the elastic inside the doll that held the arm on had snapped, but once we'd swaddled the baby in the shawl again you couldn't tell the difference. Who cared, anyway? I looked around at all the happy, smiling faces and knew that everyone's joy was all that mattered.

A Wounded Christmas

Mary Wood

DECEMBER 1942

Alice

Alice gripped her head in her hands, but the action failed to block out all her fears. Not her past, nor her time behind enemy lines working with the Resistance, nor her deep worry for her darling Steve – out there somewhere, she didn't know where . . .

For the umpteenth time she asked herself, *Is he safe? Is he alive?* And prayed, *Please God he is, and please, please keep my darling sister Gertrude safe too.*

So much to haunt her. So much to make her heart heavy. A heart that had suffered, but also found joy beyond measure in her love for Steve and in the discovery of her half-sister Gertrude.

The soft rug yielded to her feet and gave comfort

as she swung her legs off the couch. Bad things were happening everywhere, but everyone had to carry on as best they could; she would be no different. Time to reconsider her options . . . The shrill sound of the phone cracked the silence around her and interrupted her thoughts. Her body stiffened as she listened to her maid answering the call.

'Yes, Miss Alice is in, who is calling, please? Oh! Very well, please wait a moment.'

Rising in one movement, Alice opened the door to the hall just as her maid lifted her hand to knock. 'Who is it, Penny?'

'The nursing home, Miss Alice, they need to speak to you.'

Mother! Oh God!

Hearing the words spoken to her down the crackling line took the strength from her legs. Backing towards the chair that stood nearby, she sank into it and tried to speak. 'But – but . . . She was fine yesterday, she—'

As if she hadn't spoken, the matron continued in a matter-of-fact way: 'I'm afraid we don't think she has long. The doctor has just left, but he warned it may only be hours. I'm sorry.'

'I – I will come straight away.'

Brave words, but going to see her mother had always taken even more courage than she'd had to muster in the thick of the dangerous missions in France. So much hung between them: cruelty, lack of care, lies. Then there was her mother's final mental breakdown that had indirectly caused the death of dearest Bren, her closest childhood friend and someone who had wanted to be more. How sad that she hadn't been able to feel the same for him. But he died thinking she did, and that was all that mattered.

'I have your coat ready, Miss Alice, and Jensen is bringing the car around to the front for you. I hope Lady Louisa is all right.'

Dear Penny would only be paying lip service to this wish. She'd been with the family a long time and remembered what used to go on. She and Cook and the lovely Bill, their former gardener, had done what they could to protect her against Mother's violent outbursts and the vile acts of Nanny.

The door opened and a cold breeze wafted around her, camouflaging the reason for the shiver that shook her body at the thought of the loathsome Nanny, and bringing to her the fresh wintry smells of the beautiful surroundings of her home.

The wonder of the setting of this house had always given her peace. The large dwelling, elegant in its design, stood on the edge of Bexley's Danson Park in south-east London. Its garden sloped down towards the natural beauty, giving views of nature dressed in all seasons. Today, white frost clothed it, providing a spectacular vision of hedges draped in lace, and trees like dancing giant fairies, swaying proudly in their winter finery. But both were outdone by the lake, which dazzled like a thousand diamonds as the sun, low in the sky, skimmed its surface with a weak shimmering light.

A peace settled in Alice, as it always did when she allowed herself a moment to let the beauty of the scene seep into her: a landscape so at odds with what disturbed her mind and light years apart from the reality of the hell searing the real world as the war raged towards its third year.

With this inner peace came an urge to live in the now. The past was the past, the present held its own heartache, but there was still plenty to get on with. She could be of more use to her country than she was at the moment. The humdrum existence of dealing with admin at the War Office had kept her occupied, but she wanted to go back and continue the work she had begun with the Resistance. Back to Gertrude, to secure her safety. Miraculously, Alice thought, the injuries she'd sustained at the hands of the Germans, when they'd captured her and Steve, had healed.

Again she thought of Steve. Their escape, orchestrated by the Resistance movement, had resulted in further injury to him. Whether he'd recovered from that injury, she did not know. Nor did she know whether Alfonse, the leader of the movement, had been able to get himself and Steve to safety. The not knowing was a source of agony to her, and yet it held hope as she clung on to the belief that no news was good news.

But, all of that aside, she would approach the General this afternoon, no matter the outcome of this visit to her mother. She would beg him to let her go back. She had so much knowledge and training going to waste. She needed to be back in France, using her expertise to further the cause. Somehow she would persuade the powers that be that she was ready.

Lil

Lil's hand had gone numb. The face of the young officer holding it was screwed up in agony. The doctor's voice droned on in the background, soothing but useless words: 'Nearly done, old chap. The last stitch going in now. Once this is done you will feel more comfortable.'

Comfortable? Eeh, she doubted the lad would ever know the meaning of the word again. One of his legs had been blown off and half of the arm on the same side, and with some horrific internal injuries the lad was in agony. Now he had a deep gash on his good arm, brought about by his thrashing about and hitting the iron bedstead. Probably in anger. Many emotions took these lads, but anger always triumphed.

'All done, sir. You'll be reet.' Releasing her hand from his grip and wiping his face with a cool damp cloth she had at her side, Lil tried to offer encouragement. 'Come on, now, your young 'un will be in this evening to see you. Think about that and try to get yourself rested for her visit, eh?'

His 'thank you' came from lips that still grimaced with pain.

'When can I give him his next pain relief, Doctor?'

'I have made one up for him to take in fifteen minutes. It was unfortunate that this happened when his last dose was wearing off. Keep your chin up, young man, getting better is all to do with willpower.'

'Aye, and he's a lot to win through for. By, lad, your young 'un's a bonny lass, and she wants to have Christmas with her daddy. So make that happen, eh?' Lil often found herself dropping the formal address of her charges, but none of them seemed to mind.

All of her patients were officers, all broken in some way or other in the line of duty. This hospital, fashioned out of a beautiful old mansion in Kent, offered them a peaceful sanctuary to recover in – or, God forbid, to die in, with dignity and amongst their own.

Straightening her body, Lil looked out of the window. The typical English country-house garden surrounding the house looked like a winter wonderland as the frost whitened everything. Even the statues had icicle jewellery hanging from them, as if dressed in their best finery for Christmas.

In the dimming light of late afternoon, the more able-bodied officers wandered around outside, despite the cold. Tiny red lights glowed as they drew on their cigarettes. Small groups chatted, some men stood on their own. What was going through the minds of these solitary figures she could only guess.

Frustration brought a sigh from Lil. How long before the bosses of the Red Cross approved her application to work for the Voluntary Aid Detachment? She'd passed all her exams and was a fully qualified nurse now. She'd done her time in this hospital and she was ready. More than ready. Especially now that Mildred, her ma-in-law, was nicely settled in living with Gillian. What Lil would have done without Gillian, she didn't know. The lass had been her saviour and the best friend a girl could have. *Eeh, thinking of me and Mildred living down here in London at all, is a wonder. I never thought I'd leave the North, let alone that Mildred would do so! Not with how Mildred was so set in her ways.* But with Alfie – Mildred's son and Lil's late husband – not coming back from the war, there just didn't seem any reason to stay up there. Yes, it had been Lil's birthplace, the small Yorkshire town bordering Lancashire, but it didn't hold happy memories for her.

Born in a workhouse and losing her mother, who'd

succumbed to the disease and hunger that was rife in that institution, she'd found a spark of happiness at first with Alfie. But the bitterness in him at being an unrecognized bastard son of the owner of the Mill, had eroded that happiness and led to Lil suffering violence and rape at his hand.

The arrival of young Gillian, an evacuee to their area from London, had marked the turning point for her. With Alfie away, she'd accompanied Gillian to her home on a visit and had been drawn to help the folk of the stricken East End. Working with the local Red Cross had led her to take up nursing, and here she was. But her efforts still didn't feel enough. She wanted to do so much more!

As Lil raised her hand to pull down the window blind, knowing blackout time was approaching, a car swung in at the gate and made its way up the long drive towards the building. *Alice? Yes! Eeh, that's a turn-up, but a welcome one.*

Alice was the only other good thing, besides Mildred, that had come into Lil's life through her marrying Alfie. It had been Alice's uncle who had fathered Alfie. Meeting her had been a shock. Having to tell her who she was and about her husband being Alice's half-cousin hadn't been easy.

Alice had been brought into this hospital, injured and broken in spirit. Lil had known who she was as soon as she'd heard her surname. But far from the revelation causing friction, it had joined them in a loving friendship. And they had been a help to one another. Now, mended, well in body if not in mind, Alice had taken to Mildred, providing her – the woman who'd been wronged by Alice's uncle – with the means to live a good life, or at least the best anyone could as things were today. Mildred spent a few days at Alice's every week and savoured her part in taking care of Alice. Not that Alice wanted her to help, but she could see it made Mildred happy to do so.

Alice stepped out of the car and came up the steps. Her presence took this beautiful building back to its former glory – a Rolls-Royce parked at its steps with a chauffeur helping a lady to alight. It made Lil wonder, as she had done many times, what life had been like here before all of this happened. Alice had told her a little, as she had attended balls here with her then beau, Bren, but still, it was hard to imagine the place as it was. Now packed with wards and operating theatres, peopled with gliding nuns and giggling nurses, the building provided shelter and care, but also saw the toll of human misery that war had brought to it. Though, she had to admit, that was balanced with hope, and sometimes laughter from the wounded.

Completing the blackout of her ward and carrying

out a quick check of all her patients, Lil hurried to meet Alice.

'Eeh, lass, what brings you here? I wasn't expecting you . . . Oh, Alice, love, you look all in.' As she held her, she felt her dear friend's fragility. Her bones were not comfortable to hug as they had hardly any flesh on them. 'Come through to the rest room. I've a few minutes to spare afore I have to do me medicine rounds.'

A huge log fire crackled in the grate of the ornate fireplace. It was a grand room that had been set aside for the nurses to take respite in.

'Sit yourself down, lass. Warm your cockles, as Gillian would say.'

'How is Gillian? Mildred said she was full of a cold. Poor girl. Do you think she will ever get over losing her sister, and . . . well, the attack on you both?'

Alice's words shuddered the memory of Alfie's revenge through her. When he found out she had left his home, he arranged for her to be attacked and raped. Guilt seared her as it did every time she thought of how Gillian had got caught up in that attack and suffered so much. Shaking the thought away, Lil answered Alice. 'Naw, Alice, I don't think Gillian will ever get over it, but I reckon her going off after Christmas to be a Land Girl might help. I hope so. Now, don't let's talk about it. Tell me what's brought you here, as I can see all is not reet with you.'

'It's Mother. I've been to the nursing home this morning. They'd called me in and told me she hadn't got long...'

'Eeh, lass...'

'It's all right, she rallied. Oh, Lil, there is so much conflict in me where Mother is concerned, and today, when I thought I would lose her, I tried to reach out to her, but she still had no time for me.'

'I'm sorry, love, it must be hard for you. But you do reet to keep in touch with her. None of what happened is your fault, and the circumstances around the past have a lot to do with how your mam behaved, you know that.'

'But that doesn't excuse her, Lil, and what's worse is now I've found out so much about what happened to my father, in some ways Mother's behaviour is even harder to live with. Anyway, I didn't come for sympathy. I came to be with you. I have such a lot to talk over.'

'Naw, don't tell me. They haven't accepted that you want to go back into action, have they?'

'Yes, they have. I rang my superior when I got home from my visit to my mother. I begin training next week, with a view to being deployed a few weeks after Christmas.'

'Deployed at what? Can't you tell me?'

'Don't ask me, Lil, you know I can't reveal what I do, or where I will be going.'

'By, I'm sorry. Whatever possessed me? Eeh, lass, it's

so easy to let yourself down when with friends. I know I should never ask such things, but it came so natural. And that's exactly why you shouldn't tell me. But whatever it is, keep safe, love. I couldn't bear to lose thee.'

'I will. And don't worry, it was an easy slip. Now, let's talk of something else. Christmas, for instance. I mean, it is only just a week away, you know.'

'Aye, I know, but I haven't given it much thought.'

'Neither had I till today. I came away from the nursing home lifted a little in how I have been feeling lately. Mother was weak, but was out of danger, and that in itself gave me some relief. It seems she has a mild form of pneumonia. But she has a strong constitution and doesn't look anywhere near ready to go yet, thank God.'

'Nice to hear you say that, love.' It surprised Lil to realize that Alice had said this last as if she really meant it. *But then, there's nowt thicker than blood, they say.*

'I know, I can't believe how much I mean it myself. Anyway, it set me thinking and I realized so much is happening after Christmas, but asked myself, what about Christmas itself? Why don't we make the best of it that we can? Will you be free any of the days of Christmas week?'

This put a warm feeling into Lil, and marked a huge step forward for Alice. How much of that was down to her being accepted to go back to whatever it was her war effort entailed, or how much to her mother rallying, Lil didn't ask. She was too happy at the change in Alice's spirits for that to matter. 'Aye,' she told her. 'I will. It's just one, but I've been given Boxing Day off. I finish at 7 p.m. on Christmas Day night, and I don't have to be back until midday the day after Boxing Day, when I'm on a late shift. What have you in mind?'

'I haven't made any definite plans, but I thought we could all be together: you, me, Mildred and Gillian, at my house, and have the best traditional day we can have. It can be on Boxing Day, and you can all stay over. If you all come Christmas night, we can do the present-giving, then have a late fireside supper, and get up in the morning and have eggs . . .'

'Eggs! By, lass, that'll be sommat. Can you get eggs . . . ?'

'I can. My new gardener, an old man who has worked on a farm in this area all his life, has started a kind of smallholding on part of my land. He has chickens, and grows vegetables for the house, and seems to be able to get his hands on a few things that I ask no questions about. He has already said he has a broiler marked for execution for Christmas dinner . . .'

There was a moment when Lil felt repulsed by the expression Alice had used, but looking at Alice's face fit to burst with laughter she felt a giggle bubble up and let it have rein. It felt good to laugh together and with the laughter came a feeling of excitement. Christmas, and in a big house, with all her friends around her . . . *Eeh, the thought lifted her.*

And her laughter increased as Alice mimicked her way of speaking and said, 'Eeh, it'll be grand, lass. Grand as owt.'

Their fit of giggles deepened to a belly laugh that resounded around the room. A knock on the door stopped them. A young man, with a bandage over one eye and leaning heavily on a crutch, stood there looking apologetic. 'I'm sorry, the sound of merriment, like I never thought to hear ever again, drew me. It was like music to my ears.'

'And mine.' Another officer stood behind him, one arm of his pyjama top loosely tucked into his pocket. And another, then another, until there were ten or more of them all standing with a look of hunger on their faces. A hunger for laughter . . . A sad and poignant hunger.

'Well, you will hear plenty of that next week, gentlemen. We are going to have a Christmas to remember, right here in the ballroom, if we can get permission, and if you can muster enough strength to clear it and get it ready.'

This, from Alice, shocked Lil. Where did she dream that up from, and more importantly, how was she going to manage it? 'Alice?'

'It can be done. I'll find a way. In the meantime,

chaps, set to! Find any talent amongst you and organize a concert. Any talent at all – singers for a choir, jokers to make us laugh, writers to compose some verse and musicians to form a band. I'll sing a song or two, I've been known to in the past.' The wink Lil received from Alice reminded her of an unlikely evening, but a very enjoyable one, that she, Gillian, Alice and Mildred had spent at a free 'n' easy, when Alice had sung! Her being there at all had been amazing, but hearing her belt out a Vera Lynn number had topped all Lil had ever thought to see in her life. But then, war was a great leveller.

To the officers' looks of astonishment, Alice said, 'Don't worry, I'll make it happen, and I will supply everything we need, from musical instruments to food and drink. We are going to have a Christmas party, gentlemen, and put our two fingers up to Hitler.'

A cheer went up, the like of which Lil never thought to hear in this place, and it made her heart swell to see that those once haggard and fearful faces now held excitement and anticipation.

The Boxing Day Party

Alice stood with Lil and looked around the ballroom. A joint effort of many of the local businesses and the doctors and nurses had made this happen. And all the families had risen to the challenge to provide things. A phone call to Alice's old friend, Rosamond, whose parents had given this house to become a wartime hospital, had revealed that the family's Christmas decorations were still stored in the attic. Retrieving them meant that now every corner twinkled with the tiny lights that adorned bunches of holly and streamers strung from them to the centre of the ceiling. In the corner a huge tree, cut from the many in the garden, looked a picture – laden as it was with glass baubles that caught the light and reflected it around the room. Fighting sadness as memories of past times haunted her, Alice allowed only the good feeling of a mission accomplished to seep into her. Lil's words helped, as always: 'Eeh, it looks grand. It's like the war and all its misery has been shut out and a magic has taken over. Men who only knew pain and suffering and whose crying bounced off the walls at night have changed into folk with hope, whose music and chatter have replaced the tears. Their talk is all of tonight, and of being with their families again. It is wonderful how many can come. You've done that, Alice. You deserve a medal, lass.'

'Oh, no, Lil, I have gained as much as I have given, as making it all happen has helped me, too. That is thanks enough.'

Tears came again as the band struck up, but these were tears of joy shed by the families and comrades of those making the music. As Alice listened to the music – music a professional would probably scream at but which to her sounded divine – she looked along the row of chairs next to her. Gillian sat holding both Mildred's and Lil's hands, and though her cheeks were wet with crying, her expression showed a joy, something that hadn't been in her since the loss of her sister and the vile attack on her. *Everything has been worth the effort just to see that.*

On her other side, her mother sat in a wheelchair dressed in her finery and wrapped in a fox fur, even though it was warm in here, and she looked lovely. Next to her was Mother's friend, Lady Elizabeth, Bren's mother. Lady Elizabeth had never made the connection between her son's death and Mother's actions, and Alice felt glad about that as she was the only friend Mother had left from her heady days as a feted socialite. All others had snubbed her after Father had been shot as a traitor. *Don't . . . don't think about bad things!*

A voice that could only belong to Lil cut into her thoughts as the piece the band was playing came to an end. 'Reet, lads, that were grand, but can you play owt of Vera Lynn's? Come on, Alice, up you get. Eeh, you're all in for a treat. Our Alice has the voice of an angel.'

Hot with embarrassment, but thinking it better not to protest, Alice rose. A voice beside her snapped, 'Alice, don't you dare! It is so undignified!'

Freezing in a half-standing, half-sitting position, Alice was struck by her childhood fear as if a hand had slapped her. Mother's face held all the hatred of the past.

'Louisa, no. You promised you would be good if I brought you here. Alice has done all of this to give these wounded officers something special at Christmas: now don't you dare spoil that for them or for her!' Lady Elizabeth's tone had a sternness Alice had never heard the gentle woman use before.

Mother looked blank. 'What is the matter, Elizabeth? Alice? Where is Alice, is she here?'

Seeing the bewilderment and the lost look on her mother's face cut Alice in two, and she realized she'd rather have her mother angry at her and knowing it, than this confusion that encased her, not knowing from one minute to the next what she was saying, or who her daughter was.

A chant of, 'Alice, Alice,' set up.

'Go, darling. Go on. Knock them dead, as they say in showbusiness. I'll take care of your mother.'

Lady Elizabeth's encouraging smile made her mind up. As she walked towards the stage, her fears and nerves left her. She loved to sing, and this one she would sing for her Steve and darling Gertrude . . .

A silence fell as the piano played the introductory chords, then Alice felt her voice carry far beyond the rafters of this beautiful room and touch every heart in it as she sang 'We'll Meet Again'.

When she came to the second rendition of the chorus, she fixed her eyes on Mildred, Gillian and Lil and gestured to them. As they walked towards her, their voices joined hers, and a feeling of great pride filled her, to know them and to be one of them.

Yes, they were unlikely friends: she from the upper classes, Lil and Mildred from the working-class North and Gillian an East Ender, but the war had thrown them together, and it had been like finding the missing links in her life. She knew they felt just the same.

As the cheers deafened them, the girls all hugged. Someone shouted, 'Let's clear a space and dance!'

Nothing had ever warmed her heart more than seeing these broken men, helped by their wives and families to feel and look whole again as they jigged to the music in the best way they could.

She stepped down to stand beside her mother's wheelchair. A feeling of shock hit her. A hand had found hers and held it. *Mother was holding her hand!* Something she had never done in her life. Tears threatened, and she let them fall. They were a release. Gillian brought her out of them.

''Ere, love, me and Lil are going outside for a breather, you coming?'

'I'll be there in a moment.'

Mildred leaned over and said, 'You go, lass, your mother'll be fine. I'll take care of her.'

Looking from Lady Elizabeth to Mildred and then to her mother, Alice hesitated.

'Yes, run along, dear. I have my maid with me.'

This, from her mother, left Alice not knowing whether to laugh or cry, but one look at Mildred showed she didn't mind being thought of in this way. Lady Elizabeth winked and said in a low voice, 'Take it all in your stride, dear.'

Outside, the stars twinkled a welcome and the moon provided a light they didn't want to see, as, though air raids were less frequent, it was a perfect night to send out our own pilots on missions.

A roar of engines told her that was exactly what was happening. Fighter planes had taken off from Biggin Hill.

'One, two, three . . .'

'What you counting, Lil?' Gillian asked.

'The aircraft. We all do it, then we count them back in to see how many we lost. The men like to light a candle to them.'

'Let's not tonight, Lil. Let's just pray for them to all return and leave it at that. I would rather not know.'

'Aye, you're reet. Tonight is special and I know as our prayers will bring the lads home.'

A silence fell for a moment. Alice broke it. 'I'm glad you've had your acceptance, Lil, and that you are going to go to France. But I worry about you. It is so dangerous.'

'I'll be reet. We all will, I can feel it in me bones.'

'Well, I know as I'll be OK, I'm really looking forward to working as a farmhand.'

'You'll love it, Gillian. And just think, lass, you can use the manure for perfume, then you won't notice the stink.'

They all giggled at this, a giggle that turned into a belly laugh as Gillian said, 'An' I'll bottle some and keep it for you, an' I might just sell it up the market when this lot's over!'

As the laughter died down, Alice opened her arms. Both girls came into the hug and smiled up at her as she told them, 'It is ten o'clock, the hour when I look up to the stars to connect with someone very special who does the same.'

They didn't question her, but looked up with her. *Are you gazing up at this moment, my darling Steve, just as we promised each other?* Somehow, she knew he was and her heart warmed.

'You know, Alice, I'd thought of this as a wounded Christmas, but you mended it, not just for us, but for all them inside that hall. Just for a few hours, you put them together again. You're a grand lass and I love you like you were me sister.'

Lil's words were bittersweet, as she thought of her half-sister, Gertrude, but Gillian helped the feeling of sorrow to be diminished by joy as she said, 'It's a

Christmas to remember and to take us all forward. And I tell you what'd be good. Why don't we do as Alice just did? Connect, I mean. Look up at the stars whenever they are out, just before ten so that we don't interfere with Alice's special time, and think of each other. That'll bring us together wherever we are.'

'Aye, let's. That's a grand idea. And I'll never think of Christmas as wounded again, 'cos I'll always have this memory of a day of love and friendship.'

Alice could only hold them close in a moment that held all the emotions of war. A moment that was shattered as the door opened and a young officer shouted, 'Hey, what are the three best-looking girls doing out here? We need you inside, they're playing a jive. Come on, I may only have one arm, but I can show them Yanks a thing or two about dancing.'

All three, caught up in the laughter and anticipation of this, skipped up the steps, and Alice thought: *Never have I ascended these stairs so eagerly as now. And somehow I feel that Steve, and Gertrude, and yes, Bren, Bren more than any of them, are climbing them with me.*

On entering the ballroom the music whipped up that wonderful feeling inside her of freedom and expression as her body began to sway to the rhythm. Yes, there was a lot to face, but for now all demons had left her – she had mended a wounded Christmas.

A Childhood Christmas Eve Memory

MARY WOOD

THE THIRTEENTH CHILD
OF FIFTEEN CHILDREN

The table was laden with coloured crêpe paper, paste made from flour and water, and scissors. Mum cut the crêpe paper into strips and we children plaited three colours together into long chains. The fire crackled and spat angry sparks onto the rug.

A gust of wind heralded the older brothers coming in. A grotesque head dangled from a golden-feathered body – from somewhere, no one knew where, they had found a cockerel. And not only that: one of them held a sack aloft and out of it peeped holly branches heavy with berries.

Soon the excitement built. Taking it in turns to pluck the bird, the brothers then singed the remaining stubs, while we girls collected up the mounds of feathers, giggling as fun-time took over and we threw them at each other. Mum was cross, but only for a moment.

Time for a last stir of the Christmas pud –
make a wish – Oh, I do want that doll! So pretty
with its pink frock and bonnet!

Delicious smells from the oven – mince pies all
ready for Santa.

In comes Dad, all merry and singing carols.
Mum tells him off. He smiles and like a conjuror
brings out from under his coat a bottle of sherry.
The golden liquid catches the light. Mum forgives
Dad.

'Please can we put the decorations up now?'

But no. Mum will not waver from tradition.

The crib is up, a lovely cave made from crisp
brown paper with icing sugar for snow – did
it snow in Jerusalem? And twigs for trees. The
shepherds are there, and the animals, and Joseph
and Mary. Soon baby Jesus will arrive and lie in
the cradle. Then the kings will come, but that is
days away and will mark the end of Christmas, so
I don't want to think of them.

Potatoes to peel, sprouts to prepare, bacon rolls
to make, stuffing to mix – all the girls receive a
job, even the three youngest of which I am the
eldest at eight years old. Besides us three there are
four more girls and three brothers at home. Two
brothers were already married by that time with
families of their own. They would visit soon. And,

never forgotten – three brothers, unknown to me as they died before I was born. But their names were special, as we mentioned them each night in family prayers.

Time for socks. All bathed and shivering from cold, we see the socks, all in a row – what will they contain when Santa fills them and hangs them on the bottom of our bed? Ooooooooh – so excited.

Off we go. Fight over the army coats that cover us, but give in and snuggle together to keep warm – four in a bed.

Creaking door opens. Tightly close my eyes. Feeling that I will burst with a mixture of fear of the bearded man who I am convinced has entered our room, and the excitement at having presents!

Not quite dawn: we can wait no longer. Orange peel, nutshells and gold-coloured foil strew the bed. All treats devoured, and the moon is still in the sky. Feeling sick, we try to get off to sleep. Will the doll appear at the end of my bed in the morning?

The parcel is the right shape. I can hardly breathe – but no. But it doesn't matter! I have a magical set of yellow and red weighing scales! So happy. I love them!

Now it is time. We run towards the living room / kitchen of the old army hut we live in. The red tiles are cold to our feet, but we don't care. Our eyes feast on the magic of Christmas – our own grotto. Every bit of the ceiling and the top of the walls are draped with our paper chains. Tinsel hangs over it, glittering and shimmering in the light. In the corner a holly-bush Christmas tree, hung with baubles and Christmas crackers. Carols ring out from the radio. Mum greets us all with a hug. Happiness clothes me. It's Christmas Day, 1953!

More from Pan Macmillan's
Saga Authors . . .

Diane Allen

Diane Allen was born in Leeds, but raised at her family's farm deep in the Yorkshire Dales. After working as a glass engraver, raising a family, and looking after an ill father, she found her true niche in life, joining a large-print publishing firm in 1990. Rising through the firm, she is now the general manager and has recently been made Honorary Vice President of the Romantic Novelists' Association.

Diane and her husband Ronnie live in Long Preston in the Yorkshire Dales, and have two children and four beautiful grandchildren.

More Books by Diane Allen

For the Sake of Her Family
For a Mother's Sins
For a Father's Pride

FOR A FATHER'S PRIDE

by Diane Allen

In 1871, young Daisy Fraser is living in the Yorkshire Dales with her beloved family. Her sister Kitty is set to marry the handsome and dangerous Clifford Middleton. But on the eve of the wedding, Clifford commits an act that shatters Daisy's happy life and forces her to give birth to a baby she believes is dead. Soon she is cast out by her family and has no choice but to make her own way in the world.

When further tragedy strikes, Daisy sets out for the bustling streets of Leeds. There she encounters poverty and hardship but also friendship. What she really longs for is a love of her own. But the key to happiness may not be as far away as she thinks . . .

Read on for an extract from
For A Father's Pride by Diane Allen

1

Grisedale, Yorkshire Dales, 1872

The sun shone through the chapel window, the shimmering rays dancing and playing around the young couple who were taking their vows of marriage, quietly and with reverence.

Daisy Fraser watched with damp eyes as her older sister, Kitty, let her new husband tenderly slip the ring onto her finger and then kiss her gently on the cheek. She was torn between jealousy, regret and anger at herself. She should have told her sister who she was marrying: what a rat Clifford was, and that he was only after their father's money. Clifford Middleton – there he stood, the dark-haired and handsome heir to Grouse Hall, Grisedale, marrying the baker's oldest daughter, who came into the marriage with a handsome dowry. But it was young Daisy who knew what he was really like. She quickly swept away an escaping tear that was falling down her cheek. Her mother noticed, squeezed her hand and whispered, 'Never mind, dear, your day will come,' not realizing that her daughter wasn't crying out of regret.

Daisy gave a false smile. She had tossed and turned for nights, wondering whether to tell her sister, but the wedding plans had been well under way. And how could she spoil Kitty's wedding day with the most disastrous news you could hear coming from the lips of your sweet younger sister? Daisy had always lusted after Clifford. She knew he was a good-for-nothing, but his father was wealthy, he dressed in the sharpest suits and he always had a twinkle in his eye and a smile for the ladies – everything that young Daisy, at sixteen, had admired. But it had been Kitty's hand he'd asked for in marriage this spring, and Daisy had been broken-hearted at the fact that Clifford had never given her a second glance.

That was until Kitty and their mother had gone to Sedbergh for some supplies for the wedding breakfast. Daisy had been in the house alone; her father had been delivering bread over in the nearby valley of Uldale, and she'd been left to tidy up and prepare the spare room for the guests who would soon be arriving. She'd turned round quickly, sensing someone in the room with her, to find Clifford leaning against the doorway smiling at her. She could still hear his soothing, dark voice and see the way he looked commandingly at her. She could remember how he said that he was being a fool and was marrying the wrong sister, and that he would rather have

Daisy's brains than Kitty's beauty. She could remember how he'd wooed her and made her feel special, saying that at sixteen she was nearly a woman – and would she like to know what it felt like to be a true woman?

Colour rose in her cheeks as she thought of the moment when he carried her into her mother and father's bedroom, pulling up her skirts and kissing her tenderly, making her feel like a grown woman, and secretly satisfied that Clifford was showing her the lover she could be. He unbuttoned his trousers, but it was then that she'd come to her senses and pleaded with him not to go any further – to no avail. She'd pounded her fists on his chest and screamed in his ear, as he grinned wickedly at her while unbuttoning his trousers. Daisy winced aloud as he entered her, frightened but too scared to shout any more, as he roughly covered her mouth with his foul-smelling hands. He kissed her roughly, biting and scratching her, as each thrust became harder and deeper. Never had she been touched and used like that before. It was painful, and her legs and body ached. Finally he'd rolled off her, exhausted, and Daisy had lain next to him nearly in tears, realizing what she had done, overcome with pain and shame after the agony and heat of the moment had passed. She had allowed her future brother-in-law to go where no honourable gent would even mention, let alone touch – losing her virginity to a cad, someone who had no respect for her or her sister.

She'd watched as Clifford had buttoned up his trousers and grinned before saying, 'Two sisters in one day – one with money and the other without. Still, you were a good ride, Miss Fraser.' And she remembered sobbing into her mother's bedding as she pulled her skirts down, feeling used and filthy. She'd stayed in her parents' room until she heard him go down the stairs and slam the front door, and then she'd stood, with his seed running down her legs. She remembered the rush she had made to the kitchen, to wash him away; how she'd trembled with the jug full of cold water and the cloth, washing her private parts and getting rid of the smell that he'd left behind, before her parents returned.

'Daisy, are you all right, you look quite flushed? Don't they make such a beautiful couple? Kitty has done so well for herself. To think my daughter is going to be the mistress of Grouse Hall – I just can't believe it.' Martha Fraser was pink with excitement, but at the same time concerned about her younger daughter's reaction to the wedding. 'Now, we must find you a young man, perhaps a farmer's son. Or Luke Allen has a good-looking lad – perhaps you should go into Hawes one day. Two bakeries together, now that would be something!'

'Mother, I don't aim to marry. Besides, who'd have

me? Compared to Kitty, I'm plain and ordinary: too short, too plump, with mousy brown hair. We are like chalk and cheese.' Daisy came back from her thoughts quickly.

'Nonsense, you'll grow into a fine woman. You are still young, my dear. Plenty of time to look around and find the right man – at least another five years. You don't want to be sitting on the shelf when you are over twenty, though, my dear.' Martha giggled and rushed out into the aisle as the young couple made their way down the steps, stopping at the pews of their parents.

'Mrs Fraser, you look beautiful. Why, I know now where Kitty gets her looks from – they always say "Like mother, like daughter".' Clifford Middleton kissed his mother-in-law's hand, making her go a darker shade of pink with his comments.

'Now, Clifford, words are a fine thing, but you'd better look after my daughter. She's precious to me; both of them are.' Tom Fraser pulled Kitty close to him and shook Clifford's hand, little knowing that he was shaking the hand of the man who had taken advantage of his younger daughter.

'Of course I will, Mr Fraser. I love your Kitty and hope to make her a good husband, and I'll treat Daisy like the sister I never had.' Clifford smiled like a wily fox, nearly snarling at the sight of Daisy.

'Good man – you're welcome to our family. As long as

you do right by us, we'll be right by you.' Tom slapped Clifford on the back and walked up the aisle, past the few guests and relations that had been invited.

Daisy dallied at the back of the group. She didn't want to go near her new brother-in-law; in fact, she would have done anything not to have been at the wedding. But now she knew that worse was to come, as the wedding breakfast was to be held at Grouse Hall. How dare Clifford say he would treat her like a sister? You definitely didn't take your sister to bed.

'Come on, everybody, the carriages await. My father will make everyone welcome at our home. Please don't be alarmed by the way he looks – he can understand every word you say. I'm afraid that his stroke has left him unable to speak, and his face is slightly lopsided, but behind the mask is a brain that still works.' Clifford ushered everyone into the carriages, including his blushing bride, who hung on his every word and smiled as her loving husband held out his hand to assist her.

Everyone knew that old Middleton was on his way out. He'd had a stroke a few years ago, losing his speech, but had managed to retain control by writing everything down for people to read. He'd lost his wife in childbirth, when she had tried to give him another heir; both mother and baby had died, leaving a distraught ten-year-old Clifford and a grieving husband. Since then Clifford had been brought up by a housekeeper, and his father had slowly slipped into becoming the old man he now was. Soon Grouse Hall would be Clifford's, along with the four hundred acres of land and two farm cottages that were tenanted. Clifford Middleton was a good catch for anyone who could put up with his wild ways.

'What's up, Daisy, you've got a face on you that could turn milk sour?' Tom Fraser looked at his younger daughter. 'It's a wedding, not a funeral, we've been to, and you're about to fill your belly at someone else's expense, so make the most of it.' Her father scowled at Daisy. She was his favourite, a clever lass, but far too sombre and deep-thinking sometimes. He worried that her thoughts were sometimes too deep for her own good.

'I don't like Clifford. I don't want to go and see his home, or his old father.' Daisy could have cried, but she had to keep her secret.

'Well, you were all over him the other day – tha changes with the wind, lass. I thought you liked him. Or is it, happen, a bit of jealousy creeping in?' Tom made light of her mood.

'I don't think he's right for our Kitty.' Daisy had to say it.

'Hush, child. Course he's right for Kitty – she loves

him.' Martha Fraser urged her outspoken daughter to be quiet.

'Too bloody right. He's right for our Kitty. He has plenty of brass and plenty of land, which is what a father likes to hear, so you'll keep your mouth shut and make best of it.' Tom Fraser's mood changed quickly. He'd worked hard to find his daughter a good man, and it had cost him a pretty penny. He'd made sure Kitty had been seen in all the right places and in all the society papers, just for her to catch the eye of Clifford Middleton: the catch of the Dales. He wasn't going to hear any different. 'It'll be finding somebody for you that we'll have bother with now, and you don't have the looks of your sister.'

'Father, watch what you say.' Martha scowled at him as the carriage turned up the driveway of Grouse Hall.

The long, low house of Grouse Hall stood in front of them. The limestone from which it was built looked grey and dark in the dimming light, and Daisy couldn't help but notice that the windows and doors could do with a lick of paint. It was set high on the fellside of Grisedale and had wild rushes and rough fell-grass growing around it. What had been garden walls was now rubble, and nature had taken over, making its own display of wild brambles and ragged robin, which gently bobbed its frayed petals in the breeze.

Martha Fraser held her husband's hand as he helped her out of the carriage, not quite believing this was the place where her daughter was going to live. She had understood, by the way Clifford dressed and spoke, that it was a grand hall he lived in, as the name had suggested. But this was nothing more than a rambling, neglected farmhouse. She scowled at her husband. He'd known all along what the house looked like, so why hadn't he said?

Tom whispered to her, noting her disappointment, 'Don't judge a book by its cover, Martha; he's got brass in the bank.' She held his hand and smiled at the two rather grubby servants who were standing at the gate, waiting to greet their new mistress and her family.

Daisy, left to her own devices, climbed out of the carriage unaided and stood and watched as the servants bobbed and curtsied. Then she watched as they scrambled back into the house while Clifford urged them to go about their work. With tears nearly welling up in her eyes yet again, she watched as Clifford swept Kitty off her feet and carried her over the threshold of Grouse Hall, laughing and screaming, with her family and guests cheering them on. The marriage was a farce. Were they all blind, and could they not see that Clifford's twinkling eyes and easy charm were just a pretence and that he would never be faithful to her sister? She stood for a second by the rundown garden wall, admiring the view of the dale and trying to block her ill feelings from spoiling her sister's wedding day. She watched as a nesting curlew circled overhead, crying its familiar call, before landing down in the valley bottom below. She wished she could join it and not have to attend the wedding breakfast; anything was better than having to look into the dark eyes of her brother-in-law.

She felt a hand on her shoulder.

'Now, little sister, when were you thinking of joining us? Kitty is asking for you.' Clifford's grip was like a vice on her shoulder.

She shrugged her shoulder from him to loosen his grip, and walked down the path to the porch and entrance to the hall, but he caught her just as she was about to enter.

'Don't you ever say a word about what happened the other day, or I'll make life hell for your sister and ruin your father, do you hear me? After all, you were nearly begging me for it,' Clifford snarled, holding Daisy's wrist tightly, before releasing it as one of the wedding guests strolled by the doorway.

'I'll not say anything, but you be kind to our Kitty, for she loves you.' Daisy turned her back on Clifford and entered the low, beamed home of the Middletons.

She stared at the shape of Tobias Middleton, sitting in his chair watching the wedding-party visitors come and go around him, grunting his greetings to them. She couldn't help but feel a little sorry for him, as his son completely ignored him, choosing to flirt and chat with his new in-laws and relations. She watched Tobias for a while as he tried to converse with people and then looked lost, as people gave up being polite once they couldn't understand him. She felt a bit like old Tobias herself – out of place and an outcast – and decided to sit next to him. He grunted his greeting as she introduced herself. He smiled a slow smile and took a chalk board and some chalk from next to him, before starting to write a few words very shakily. Daisy picked up the board and scrutinized it as he pushed her arm, urging her to read what was written on it. The writing was hardly legible, due to his shaky hand, but she could just make out the word 'BASTARD' written in the centre. Her face must have given her thoughts away, as the old man nudged her and pointed at his only son. She didn't reply, but Tobias Middleton nodded his head in agreement as if he knew her thoughts.

On seeing the old man laughing with Daisy, Clifford raced across the room. 'Now, Father, what are you up to? Time for your midday nap, I think. I'll call Violet, to take you into the other room.' But the old man was too fast for him, and his written thoughts about his son were quickly erased by a wipe of his jacket sleeve. Tobias grunted his objections and flayed his arms in protest. 'Now, Father, stop it, or else I'll have to tie you in your bed. You will go in the other room, for you are disturbing the guests. Violet, take him away.' Clifford raised his voice, shouting at the small dark-haired maid who cowered as she wheeled the old man out of the room. 'Sorry, everyone, my father gets a bit excited if he sees too many people. Time for him to have a nap.' Clifford calmed his agitated audience and gave a long, dark stare at Daisy.

'Poor Clifford, it must be an awful strain on him, looking after his father in such a state. He must be a saint. The dirty old man – did you see him dribbling? I couldn't believe it when you sat next to him, Daisy. Surely you have more pride?' Martha Fraser lifted her teacup to her lips, curling her small finger like royalty, as she sat next to her daughter.

Daisy looked at her. Why did her mother put on airs and graces, and think that she was better than Tobias? They were bakers, for God's sake, in the middle of the Dales – nothing special, just ordinary folk like the Middletons.

The wedding breakfast seemed to go on for an age, but at last the sun was disappearing over Baugh Fell, and with that came the announcement from Tom Fraser that tomorrow was another working day and that a baker rose early to make his money. Daisy was thankful, but held Kitty tight as she bade her farewell at the ramshackle garden gate.

'You take care; you know where home is, and that I love you.' Daisy squeezed her radiant sister tightly, tears filling her eyes as she held her hand. They weren't the closest of sisters, but she did love Kitty, and the guilt that Daisy was feeling was beginning to gnaw away at her as she bade her sister farewell.

'Don't be silly, little sis. Clifford will take care of me now, but I will miss you all.' Kitty grabbed the arm of her new husband and blew her younger sister a kiss, as Daisy climbed into the carriage that trundled down the rough path back up to the head of Grisedale.

Daisy sat quietly in the carriage, listening to her mother making plans for Kitty's future family and hoping that she'd soon be a grandmother. Daisy could think of nothing worse than her sister giving birth to children by the bastard she now knew Clifford to be, and prayed that her sister would be safe with the letch.

2

Two months had passed since the wedding and now life was back to the everyday running of the small but busy business at Mill Race. Daisy stood at the back door of the bakery. Both ovens were filled with loaves of bread, and she was about to start on the pastries and cakes. Her father had baked the first batch of bread and had long since left the small, hot bakehouse, striding out across the fell and walking up the so-called 'Coal Road' to the open-cast mine set between Garsdale and Dentdale. There he traded his freshly baked bread, cheese, and ham from his own butchered pigs. The money was good, and an extra income for the family, which made the hard slog of the walk worthwhile.

This was Daisy's only chance to take a few minutes out from her day, and from helping her family. Her mother was milking in the dairy, and the house and bakery were empty apart from her. It was still only 6 a.m., but she felt as if she had been up for an age. She'd tossed and turned all night in her bed, while a silent niggle played on her mind. She'd missed her monthly, for the first time since she'd started being a woman, and now she was beginning to worry. She might only be sixteen but, having been brought up in the country, she knew all too well what happened when opposite sexes were put together. She prayed that the one fateful time, eight long weeks ago now, when Clifford Middleton had raped her he'd not left her with child. The consequences would be devastating to her family, especially for Kitty. She had heard Clifford and Kitty talk of the family they planned, and for Daisy to be bearing his child would ruin their plans and cast dark shadows over both families.

Fighting back welling tears, she sniffed and wiped her nose with the back of her hand. There was no need to cry yet – she might just be late. After all she'd been helping her father a lot more than usual, and she was probably just tired. With brighter thoughts in her head now, she smiled as she watched a mother blue-tit bring her new family to the back door of the bakehouse to look for crumbs. The little chicks were not yet showing their full colour, with the odd fluffy feather looking out of place.

'There you go, Mam: a few crumbs for your brood; you've got a right handful there.' Daisy threw a handful of bread from the pine kitchen table and stood back as the mother bird and her brood tiptoed nearer, pecking delicately at the crumbs and then flying into a nearby honeysuckle bush.

'Talking to yourself, Daisy? Is that second batch of bread out yet, and have you started those apple pies, ready for the market in the morning?' Martha Fraser shouted out the orders as she quietly entered the room and poured the day's milk through muslin, to catch any dirt that might be in it, then stood at the sink of the bakery.

'They need another minute or two.' Daisy turned and started to rub the fats for the pastry into the flour, without thinking; she'd been baking since she was barely able to talk, and it was second nature to her. She looked at her mother. Dare she say anything to her, while they were alone? Dare she speak of things that were private and usually went undiscussed in the Fraser household?

'I'm not going to the market with you tomorrow. Kitty has sent word she wants to see me, so perhaps it's good news.' Martha scrubbed the bread board, before sighing and looking longingly out of the kitchen window. 'You never know, there may be a baby on the way, but it's early days yet. Still, I live in hope.' She carried on cleaning her dairy utensils without turning to look at Daisy. 'You'll have to go with your father tomorrow. You can drop me off on the way down to Sedbergh with the horse and cart.'

Daisy patted the pastry dough hard, the flour rising into a fine cloud as she let it fall from the huge earthenware bowl. It was no good – she couldn't keep her worries to herself any longer. She let out a sob as the pastry hit the pine table, her hands caked with sticky pastry.

'Daisy, what on earth is wrong with you? You've been acting strange since Kitty's wedding. You shouldn't be so jealous of your sister – someone will come along for you.' Martha stopped her scouring and looked across at her daughter, who was clearly upset. 'Now come on, let's get this bread out of the ovens, before your father gets back.' She looked at her younger daughter. She found it hard to talk to Daisy, for she wasn't as open-hearted as her firstborn, and showing emotion towards her was difficult.

'Mam, I need to talk. I need to talk now, before my father comes back.' Daisy pleaded with her eyes.

'Well, I'm listening. Get on with it!' Martha opened the big oven doors and pulled the first few loaves of bread out, nearly burning her fingers as she placed them on the shelves to cool.

'I'm late, Mam. You know – it's what we don't talk about.' Daisy sobbed, not daring to look at her mother.

'Aye, lass, you're young; you'll just be settling down into your stride. That'll be nothing to worry about – you've not been with a fella, so you'll be fine.' Martha sighed and pulled the last batch of bread out of the oven, patting the bottom of it to test it, not bothering even to look at Daisy's face. 'I was all over the place when I was your age.' She placed the bread on the shelf, then turned to look at her daughter, whose fretful face told her everything.

Daisy's face was red with tears and betrayed her anxiety.

'You've not, have you, Daisy – you've not been with a man? Your father will kill you, and me, if you have. He'll make our lives hell, you know that?' Martha felt sick. She knew the answer already. She'd had a sulky daughter for the last eight weeks, now that she thought about it. It made sense, what with Daisy's moods and the odd comment when she'd mentioned wanting to be a grandmother. Martha felt herself flush from head to toe with fear at how her husband would react. She knew Tom Fraser would never handle the shame of his youngest, most precious daughter being with child. Daisy was his favourite, and the apple of his eye. He boasted about her to friends, saying that Kitty was bonny, but Daisy had the brains. Martha knew he'd never be able to handle it. Sex outside marriage was not even thought about, let alone practised. In fact anything in that department was simply not talked about, full stop.

'I'm sorry, Mam, I couldn't stop him. He'd done it before I knew, and besides, I couldn't say no to Clifford.' Daisy thought her heart was going to burst; the sobs filled her throat, and she felt sick as she tried to explain. 'I'm sorry, Mam, I'm sorry. I know he's Kitty's . . . I couldn't stop him.' The words tumbled out of her mouth between breaths.

'Clifford! You mean, Kitty's Clifford? Bloody hell, lass. This gets worse by the second. Oh my God, the shame! Your father will go mad, and Kitty's trying for a bairn and having no luck. And there you are, pregnant by him. It couldn't get much worse! We're ruined, that's what we are.' Martha sat down at the table and watched her bawling daughter. 'Shut your mouth, girl! You fluttered your eyelashes at him all the time he was courting Kitty – well, you've certainly got what you deserved.'

Martha's face was flushed with anger and embarrassment, and with fear at having to tell her husband. She quickly gave a glance out of the window as she heard the noise of the garden gate.

'Get yourself out of here. Your father's coming up the path – I'll have to choose my moment to tell him.' Martha knocked Daisy out of the way and started to roll the pastry. Daisy ran out of the back door. It was one thing telling her mother, but quite another telling her father. He loved her dearly, but he ruled the family with a rod of iron.

She ran up through the yard. The family's goose gave its alarm call as she sped through the yard and up the outside steps that led to the tack room and the storage room for flour and seasonal fruit. There she threw herself onto a pile of hessian sacks and sobbed to herself. She wanted to die. Even worse, she wished the baby inside her would die. She curled up and rocked her body. What was she to do? She had nowhere to go. Nobody would give a pregnant lass house-room; not even the workhouse would want her. The cat that had been asleep in the window stretched its back and yawned, showing all its discoloured teeth, before walking casually across to her and winding its body round her arms, nudging its head against hers. Daisy pulled it towards her and held the furry, purring body close, stroking the cat's chin, as it appreciated being loved.

'Smoky, what am I going to do? I wish I could die.' Tears poured down on the grey fur of the cat as it purred its sympathy. 'I wish I'd never set eyes on Clifford Middleton. Look what he's done to me!'

'Have you made sure we have everything?' Tom Fraser looked at his youngest lass as he checked that the harness was tight. 'You look pasty this morning – what's wrong with you?' He stood tall and proud at the side of his horse, watching his daughter as she finished loading the cart for Sedbergh. He was a tall man of six foot or more, clean-shaven, with wisps of white hair showing from below his chequered cap. He talked as straight as a clean-living man should, and his clear blue eyes never missed a thing.

'I'm all right, Father.' Daisy couldn't look at him. She knew the shame he was going to feel and was dreading the consequences. She knew that Tom was usually a calm man, but she'd also seen him in a rage, when he'd taken on the world and won.

'Tell your mother we're ready. I don't know what's wrong with you womenfolk this morning. I can't make head nor tail of her, either. I swear she never slept a wink last night.'

The journey down to Sedbergh was silent. Martha Fraser sat nervously next to her husband, her head spinning with the knowledge that Daisy's predicament could not be kept hidden forever and that she would have to tell him sooner or later. The big question was whether she would tell Tom who the father was? It would mean shame for Kitty, and she dreaded to think what her husband would do to Clifford Middleton. Soon they were at the end of the lane leading to Grouse Hall. Tom pulled on the horse's reins and brought them to a halt.

'I can take you all the way up, if you want. We are in good time.' Tom lifted his wife down from the buckboard.

'No, get on your way. The earlier you are, the more trade you'll get. Besides, it'll do me good to stretch my legs.' Martha gave Daisy a nervous glance as she picked her skirts up and made her way along the dusty path.

Daisy felt her stomach churn. She was alone with her father, and all morning she'd felt sick with worry: had her mother said anything? She couldn't have done, for he was acting too normal.

'Tha's quiet, lass, what's up?' Tom looked at his youngest. She was dark and plain, but her heart was true. Not as flighty as her sister, and a better baker he'd never known; his business would be in good hands, if it were left to her. With a bit of luck he could do that. Clifford Middleton had enough brass for Kitty and any family that she might have with him. He patted Daisy's hand and smiled at her. She looked worried and had made herself scarce all day yesterday, for some reason. Perhaps she'd fallen out with her mother. 'Never mind, keep it to yourself. I don't want to know what you women get up to.' He grinned and pushed his team into a trot.

Daisy kept silent on her trip down the dale. It was a beautiful late-spring day, without a cloud in the sky. The rolling fells of the Howgills looked like velvet, as the valley opened out to reveal the small village of Sedbergh. She wished her mind was as calm as the day; it was a-swim with worry at the thought of her predicament. They entered the village to the usual greetings and pulled up in the historic marketplace, her father quickly setting out their wares, leaving Daisy to sell them while he stabled the horses and talked to his fellow traders and friends. Business went well. The Frasers had a good reputation for tasty bread and satisfying food, and by lunchtime their stall was nearly empty. Daisy enjoyed the banter; trading was all about making friends and hearing the gossip – and how much your skills were valued. It had helped settle her nerves for a few hours, and she smiled as her father praised her way with the customers. She loved him dearly; she felt closer to her father than her mother. He was quiet and steady, unlike her mother, who continually wanted a better life and was never satisfied.

'Away, lass, let's get back home.' Tom folded up the wooden stall onto the back of the cart and turned to look at his daughter. 'Tha looks white, are you sure you're all right?'

'I'm fine, just a little tired. We were up early this morning.' In truth, Daisy felt sick. She could feel a wave of nausea coming over her, and her head was light and her body wanted to give in. She heard her father's voice getting fainter as she tried to pull herself up onto the cart's seat; the blood rushed to her head, making her feel dizzy, before she collapsed and fainted in front of the market crowd.

'Out the way – make way, my lass is ill.' Tom parted the concerned crowd and lifted his daughter's head. 'Aye, Daisy, what's wrong? You've looked bad for weeks.' He held her tight, while someone passed him a drink of water from the nearby fountain to revive her. Daisy spluttered as he forced the water into her mouth. 'There, lass, don't move. I'll lie you down in the back of the cart and then I'll take you up to the doctor.' Tom put his strong arm around his daughter in an attempt to pick her up.

'No, no.' Daisy, her head spinning, struggled to come to her senses. 'I'm just tired, I'm fine.' She grabbed her father's arm and eased herself up onto her legs, still feeling queasy. 'See, I'm grand.'

'Tha doesn't look too grand to me.' Tom helped his daughter to the cart, assuring the gathering crowd they were all right and that they could all go about their own business. He didn't like folk knowing their business.

'I'm fine.' Daisy sat next to her father, feeling shaky and guilty. She knew he was going to have to be told shortly, because this was just the start of her pregnancy and she couldn't fain being tired forever.

Tom looked at his pale daughter and whipped his horses into action. He'd have words with Martha when he got home; she'd happen get to the bottom of it. Perhaps they'd been working her too hard since Kitty left.

Daisy lay in her bed cocooned by the warm feather mattress. Her heart was beating fast as she listened to her father going through his nightly ritual: the back door bolt being slammed, the grandfather clock's chain being wound slowly and carefully until the weight was at the top of the mechanism, the door of the case being carefully closed afterwards. The things she heard every night of her life, but never feeling the way she did tonight. She counted his steps in her mind. The third step always creaked and then she watched for the candlelight to pass her closed doorway. She listened through the age-old walls, too thick to hear normal conversation, but too thin to keep out the raised voices tonight. Daisy screwed her eyes tightly shut, hating the noises from her parents' room. She knew her mother was telling her father about her. Her father's voice rose with anger, and her mother was screaming at him. Daisy had broken his heart, and she knew it. The rumble of angry voices went on for hours and she cried lonely tears as she tried to sleep, eventually pulling her pillow over her head to cut out the noise. She hated the baby she was carrying; she hated Clifford Middleton; and most of all she hated herself for being so shallow with her affections.

When the early morning light broke through Daisy's bedroom window she shook herself from sleep, but immediately the despair of the previous evening swamped her again as soon as her senses awoke. Did she dare enter the bakery and act normally, or should she stay in her room? She walked across the bare floorboards and poured cold water from the wash jug into the matching bowl, freshening her face. She felt drained as she pulled on her skirts while sitting on the edge of her bed, lingering there, not wanting to confront her parents.

'You needn't bother coming down today. Your father doesn't want to see you. I've to lock you in your room, because he'll not be responsible for his actions.' Martha Fraser stood in the doorway. She was quiet – too quiet for her nature.

Daisy hid her head in her hands, before raising her tear-filled eyes to look at her mother. 'What's he like, Mam? He's not going to cause bother for our Kitty, is he?'

'Nay, he'll not be bothering them. I didn't tell him who'd fathered your bastard bairn, and it's enough that we've one daughter in disgrace, without having two in bother. You'll not say a word to him about Clifford either, else by God I'll kill you and the baby myself.' Martha looked dark and forbidding. 'I'll fetch you something to eat later, when I've time. I'm doing two folks' work this morning, thanks to you.'

With that she slammed the bedroom door shut, turning the heavy iron key in the lock and leaving a heartbroken Daisy sobbing on her bed.

Rita Bradshaw

Rita Bradshaw was born in Northamptonshire, where she lives today. At the age of sixteen she met her husband – whom she considers her soulmate – and they have two daughters and a son, and several grandchildren. To her delight, Rita's first novel was accepted for publication and she has gone on to write many more successful novels since then.

As a committed Christian and passionate animal lover her life is full, but she loves walking her dogs, reading, eating out and visiting the cinema and the-atre, as well as being involved in her church and animal welfare.

More Books by Rita Bradshaw

Alone Beneath the Heaven
Reach for Tomorrow
Ragamuffin Angel
The Stony Path
The Urchin's Song
Candles in the Storm
The Most Precious Thing
Always I'll Remember
The Rainbow Years
Skylarks at Sunset
Above the Harvest Moon
Eve and Her Sisters
Gilding the Lily
Born to Trouble
Forever Yours
Break of Dawn
Dancing in the Moonlight
Beyond the Veil of Tears

BEYOND THE VEIL OF TEARS
by Rita Bradshaw

Fifteen-year-old Angeline Stewart is heartbroken when her beloved parents are killed in a coaching accident, leaving her an only child in the care of her uncle.

Naive and innocent, Angeline is easy prey for the handsome and ruthless Oswald Golding. He is looking for a rich heiress to solve the money troubles his gambling and womanizing have caused.

On her wedding night, Angeline enters a nightmare from which there is no awakening. Oswald proves to be more sadistic and violent than she could ever have imagined. When she finds out she is expecting a child, Angeline makes plans to run away and decides to take her chances fending for herself and her baby. But then tragedy strikes again . . .

Read on for an extract from
Beyond the Veil of Tears by Rita Bradshaw

Preface

It was the smell that brought her to herself, a nauseating odour that the stronger stench of bleach and disinfectant couldn't quite mask. She began to struggle again as they half-walked, half-carried her along the green-tiled, stone-floored corridor, desperately trying to rise above the deadening stupor that had resulted from the injection administered some time before in the carriage, when she wouldn't stop fighting.

How could this be happening to her? How could she have been manhandled out of her own home in broad daylight?

She was still weak from the complications that had followed in the wake of the miscarriage, but fear poured strength into her limbs. She kicked out wildly, and one of the men dragging her growled a curse as her shoe made sharp contact with his shinbone. They came to a brown-painted door and the same man knocked twice. Although her body was aching and bruised from the fight she had put up when they had come for her, and she felt sick and dizzy, she continued to twist and wrestle against the hard hands, and screamed with all her might.

The door was opened by a stout woman in a grey dress and a starched white apron and cap. For a moment she felt a flood of relief at the sight of one of her own sex. Surely this woman would listen to her? She wasn't mad – they would see that and understand this was a terrible mistake.

'You've got yourselves a right handful with this 'un,' the man she'd kicked muttered morosely to another woman sitting behind a large polished walnut desk. As she rose to her feet and stared disapprovingly, he added, 'Carryin' on somethin' wicked, she's been. I'm black an' blue.'

The woman ignored him. Looking over his shoulder to the third man who had been following in their wake, she said, 'What medication have you administered, Dr Owen?'

'She's been on bromide and ergot for the last weeks, but I had to administer morphia on the way here, such was her agitation. I dare not give more for some hours, Matron.'

The matron nodded, then inclined her head at the other two burly uniformed females in the room, who stepped forward and relieved the men of their prisoner. Their grip was every bit as powerful as that of their male counterparts.

Granite-faced, the matron said coldly, 'Do you understand why you are here? The court has issued a lunacy order, on the grounds that you are of unsound mind following a recent malady. If you do not cooperate, my staff will be forced to use the necessary restraints to prevent injury to yourself or other persons, and that will not be pleasant.'

They weren't going to help her. She stared into the gimlet eyes, and a terror that eclipsed her previous fear caused her ears to ring. She may well have lost her reason in the minutes that followed, because she couldn't remember much of what happened, only that she fought until they thrust her into the padded cell. A number of women held her down and stripped her to her shift and drawers, before pulling a rough linen frock over her head and strapping her into a straitjacket – the white, stained, leather-covered walls and the floor packed with straw deadening any sound.

And then they left her to the hell that had opened and engulfed her.

PART ONE

A Lamb to the Slaughter

1890

Chapter One

Angeline Stewart stood in the swirling snowflakes that the bitter north-east wind was sending into a frenzied dance, but her velvet-brown eyes did not see what they were looking at. The bleak churchyard, the black-clothed figures of the other mourners and Reverend Turner standing at the head of the double grave had faded away. In their place were her beloved mother and father, as they had looked that last evening. It had only been a severe head-cold that had prevented her from accompanying them to the theatre, otherwise she, too, would most likely have been killed in the accident that ensued after they left the Avenue Theatre and Opera House in the midst of one of the worst snow blizzards Sunderland had experienced in years. The overturned coach had been found early the next morning after their housekeeper, Mrs Lee, who was also the coachman's wife, had instigated a search after they'd failed to return. Her parents and the coachman were dead, pinned be-neath the badly smashed coach. It had veered off the road and down an embankment, and the two horses had been so badly injured that they had been shot at the scene.

Angeline brushed a strand of burnished brown hair from her cheek and took a deep breath against the picture that her mind conjured up. She hadn't been allowed to see her parents after the accident. Her Uncle Hector, her father's brother, had forbidden it after he had identified the bodies. He said she must remember them as they had been. He wasn't to know that her imagination presented her with horrors probably far worse than the reality, images that caused her to lay awake most nights muffling her sobs.

'All right, m'dear?'

Her uncle squeezing her arm brought her back to the present, the moment before Reverend Turner beckoned them forward so that she could drop the two long-stemmed red roses she was holding on top of the oak coffins that had been lowered into the earth. Red roses had been her dear mama's favourite flowers, and McArthur – their gardener – had kept the house supplied with fragrant blooms winter and summer, courtesy of the heated greenhouses that were his pride and joy.

Angeline glanced at him as she passed the group of servants she regarded as family. McArthur's weather-beaten face was grim and his two lads, Seth and Bernie, who assisted their father in the upkeep of the two acres of land surrounding the house on the edge of Ryhope, had no cheeky smiles today. Myrtle, the house-maid, Lottie, the kitchen maid, and Mrs Davidson, the cook, were openly crying; and even Fairley, her father's butler-cum-valet, was struggling to keep back the tears. And poor Mrs Lee, who was standing with Angeline's governess, Miss Robson, looked about to faint.

Angeline paused at the woman's side and touched her arm. She'd wanted the interment of the house-keeper's husband to be incorporated in the service for her parents, but her uncle wouldn't hear of the idea, saying it wouldn't be seemly for a mere servant to be given such regard. She had tried to argue with him, but when Reverend Turner had agreed with her uncle, she had been forced to admit defeat. Simon Lee would be buried tomorrow, and his widow would have to endure a second funeral.

Her uncle's hand in the small of Angeline's back urged her forward. The subtle pressure had the effect of making her want to resist. Her father would have seen nothing wrong in publicly expressing empathy towards their housekeeper, who had been with her parents even before she was born. He'd always maintained that it was their duty to care for and protect their servants, and that each should be treated as a valued human being. She had grown up knowing that her father's father had been born in the slums of Sunderland's notorious, disease-ridden East End. Her grandfather had escaped by running away to sea at an early age, returning a rich man at the age of forty. After setting up as a wine and spirit merchant, he'd married the daughter of a local jeweller. Exactly how he had acquired his wealth was never discussed, and she had been forbidden to ask any questions on the subject by her mother, but she did know that when her grandmother had died giving birth to her Uncle Hector, ten years after her father had been born, her grandfather had wanted nothing to do with his younger son. She'd thought that very unfair.

'Come along, my child.'

Reverend Turner was holding out his hand to her and she stepped forward. She didn't like the Reverend. She had once heard her mother describe him to her father as a cold fish, when they hadn't thought she was listening, and she'd thought this a very apt description. The minister always had cold, clammy hands even on the hottest day, and his pale-blue bulbous eyes and fat lips reminded her of the rows of gaping faces in the fishmonger's window. She had said this once to her mama, and although her mother had reprimanded her, her eyes had been twinkling.

She bit harder on her lip as her heart and soul cried out, 'Mama, oh, Mama', but not a sound emerged. Her uncle had warned her that, out of respect for her parents, she had to conduct herself with dignity and propriety today, as befitted a young lady of fifteen years. Shows of emotion were vulgar and were only indulged in by the common people who knew no better. She had wanted to say that they were only a step removed from the common people, and that if her grandfather hadn't made his fortune, her father and uncle would most likely have been born in the East End instead of a grand house; but, of course, she hadn't. Mainly because she always felt sorry for her Uncle Hector. It must have been awful growing up knowing that your own father didn't like you and, furthermore, blamed you for your mother's death. Her grandfather had died long before she was born – her parents had been married for more than twenty years before she'd made an appearance, and her mama had often told her they'd given up hope of having a child – and in his will he had left everything to her father. Uncle Hector hadn't even been mentioned. It was as though he'd never existed.

Angeline's thoughts caused her to reach out and take her uncle's arm as they stood together, and she gave him one of the roses to throw on her father's coffin. Knowing what she did, it had always surprised her that her father and uncle got on so well, but then that was mainly due to her father. He had loved and protected his sibling all his life, and when their father had died, he'd set Uncle Hector up in his own business so that he could be independent and not beholden to anyone. Her father had been so kind, so good. Everyone said so.

When the first clods of earth were dropped on the coffins, Angeline felt as though the sound jarred her very bones. She had the mad impulse to jump into the hole, lie down and tell the grave-diggers to cover her, too. The shudder that she gave caused her uncle to murmur, 'Remember what I said, Angeline. People are looking at how you conduct yourself today.' Then he added, in a gentler tone, 'It's nearly over now. Hold on a little longer.'

The drive back to the house in Ryhope was conducted in silence. Angeline sat with her uncle and her governess in the first carriage, drawn by four black-plumed horses, followed by a procession of other carriages and conveyances. Drenched with misery, she stared unseeing out of the window of the coach. She'd always liked snow before this last week. It was so pretty, and she'd enjoyed taking walks in the winter with her mother, snug in her fur coat and matching bonnet. When they returned home they always thawed out in front of the blazing fire in the drawing room, with Mrs Davidson's hot buttered muffins and cocoa.

She hated the snow now, though. It had taken her parents, and she didn't know how she would bear the pain of their passing. It seemed impossible that she'd never see them again. Never feel her mother's arms around her or the touch of her soft lips. Never hear her father's cheerful call when he came home in the evening.

She choked back a sob, mindful of her uncle's words.

It was going to take every bit of her remaining strength to get through the next stage of the day, and she couldn't break down now. That luxury would have to wait until she was alone in her bed. Her uncle had invited friends and family back to the house for a reception following the church service, and she was dreading it. Not that there would be many family members; it would be mostly friends of her parents and business associates of her father. When her grandfather had returned to the town after being at sea, he had severed all connections with his siblings and other family members, going so far as to change his surname. Her mother had been an only child and, apart from two ancient spinster great-aunts on her side, there was no one else. No one but Uncle Hector.

She glanced at him, but he, too, was staring out of the window and seemed lost in thought. She wondered if he would go back to his own house tonight, now that the funeral was over. He had been staying with her since her parents' accident, and had seen to the arrangements for the service and other matters. This had included organizing for Miss Robson – who had previously come to the house every morning for a few hours, to take her through her lessons – to take up temporary residence and sleep in the room next to hers. This had been an added trial. She liked Miss Robson, but found her very stiff and proper, which was probably why her uncle had considered the governess an ideal companion and chaperone.

Angeline's bow-shaped mouth pulled uncharacteristically tight. She wasn't a baby. She was fifteen years old, and her father had always said she possessed an old head on young shoulders. She knew some girls of her age were flibbertigibbets and given to fancies, but she wasn't like that, possibly because her parents had had her so late in life that all their friends' children were grown-up, and so she had mixed almost entirely with adults. It would have been different if she had been allowed to go to the local school, but her father had been against it, and her mama had been equally against sending her away to boarding school. Hence Miss Robson. Not that she had minded. She loved her home and being with her mother; her mama had been her best friend and confidante and companion. Some afternoons on their walks they had laughed and laughed until their sides ached.

This time a sob did escape, and Angeline turned it into a cough. If she could just get through this day she would be able to take stock. She felt as though she had been in a daze since the accident.

Nevertheless, in spite of her desolation, as the carriage swept through the heavy wrought-iron gates and drove up the long drive to where the house sat nestled between two giant oak trees, she felt a moment's comfort. Her parents had loved Oakfield House, and so did she. She had been born in one of the eight bedrooms and had never known another home. As the family business started by her grandfather had continued to go from strength to strength, her father could have moved to a much grander house, or so her mother had confided, but both their hearts had been firmly at Oakfield. The main building consisted of fourteen rooms over two floors, with a corridor from the kitchen leading to the purpose-built annexe housing the indoor servants. McArthur and his lads lived with his wife and the rest of the family somewhere in Bishopwearmouth. Angeline didn't know exactly where, but every morning the gardener and his lads were working before she came downstairs, and in the summer they often didn't leave until twilight.

It was a happy household. Or it had been, Angeline amended in her mind as the carriage stopped at the foot of the steps leading to the intricately carved front doors. Now nothing could be the same again.

Somehow she got through the endless reception. Her new black dress with its stiff little raised collar and long buttoned sleeves seemed stifling, and the corset that

Myrtle had laced her into that morning was too tight. She had rebelled against going into corsets when she had turned fourteen, but her mother had told her that she was a young lady now and, along with privileges such as joining her parents when they had guests for dinner, there were sacrifices. Her childhood was behind her, and young ladies *always* had tiny waists. Her mama had brooked no argument on the matter, and that had been that.

Outside the house the overcast January day was bitterly cold with a keen north-east wind; inside, the huge fires burning in the basket grates of the dining room and drawing room where the hundred or so guests were assembled made the heat suffocating, at least in Angeline's opinion. All she wanted was some fresh air, or to get into a room that wasn't full of people. Nevertheless, she did her duty. She chatted here and there, accepted the words of condolence from this person and that, and behaved with the decorum her mother would have expected.

Finally, as the magnificent grandfather clock in the hall chimed four o'clock, the last of the company made their goodbyes and stepped into the snowy night. All, that is, but Mr Appleby, her father's solicitor. Before this day Angeline had only known him as a friend and dinner guest of her parents, and on those occasions she had loved to sit and listen when her father and Mr

Appleby had engaged in sometimes heated debates about social inequality and the like. These had usually finished with Mr Appleby calling her father a Socialist at heart – something her father hadn't minded in the least.

Angeline had always thought Mr Appleby's name suited him very well. Small and fat, with rosy red cheeks and twinkling brown eyes, she imagined that if an apple could take human form it would be exactly like the solicitor. Now, though, his eyes were full of sympathy when he said, 'Your uncle wishes me to acquaint you with the details of the will, Angeline', and he glanced at Hector, who was standing to the side of her.

'Now?' She asked the question of her uncle. He nodded.

'It is customary on the day of interment,' he said briefly.

Angeline didn't care if it was customary or not. She didn't want to think about the will – not today. All she wanted was to curl up by herself in front of the fire in her bedroom and cry. 'Can't it wait, Uncle Hector? I'd like to rest before dinner.'

If her uncle noticed the break in her voice, he ignored it. 'You have to understand the situation in which you find yourself, Angeline, and hear your father's instructions. It will pave the way for the arrangements that need to be made.'

She stared at him. Something told her that she

wouldn't like these arrangements. 'Do you know what the will says?'

'Partly. Your father made me your guardian, in the event of something happening to him and your mother. This was a long time ago, just after you were born. Now, please, come along to the study, where Mr Appleby has the papers ready.'

It was a moment before she followed her uncle, Mr Appleby making up the rear. Angeline's head was whirling. It was stupid, but she hadn't thought about anyone being her guardian. She'd imagined that, once the funeral was over and her uncle and Miss Robson returned to their own homes, things would get back to normal.

Well, not normal, she corrected herself in the next moment. Things would never be normal again. How could they be? But if she had thought about the future at all – which she had to admit she hadn't really, not with her mother and father filling every waking second – she'd assumed that Miss Robson would resume coming to the house in the mornings, and Mrs Lee and the other servants would run Oakfield as they always had done.

The familiar smell of woodsmoke from the fire and the lingering aroma of the cigars her father had favoured made her bite her lip as she entered the book-lined study. It was perhaps her favourite room of the house. From a little girl, she had stretched out on the thick rug in front of the fire and played quietly with her dollies, or had drawn or read books while her father worked at his desk, and as she'd grown she'd brought her needlework or crocheting and had sat in one of the armchairs at an angle to the fireplace. Her father was away so much in the town dealing with the business, and when he was home she liked to be with him, if she could. She had known that he liked having her there, albeit as a silent presence. Why had she never realized just how wonderful life was, before the accident? She'd taken it for granted, and now she couldn't tell them they'd been the best parents in the world and she loved them so much.

George Appleby walked over to her father's desk and sat down, as she and her uncle seated themselves in the two chairs that had been drawn close to it. He said nothing for a moment, his gaze on Angeline's face. He felt he knew what she was thinking, for her tear-filled eyes spoke for her, and his shock and sorrow at his dear friend's untimely death were compounded by his anxiety and concern for this young girl. Philip and Margery had been devoted to her of course, but in that devotion had come a desire to keep Angeline wrapped in cotton wool.

It was understandable – oh, indeed. He mentally nodded at the thought. They had been over the moon when they'd discovered Margery was expecting a baby, and when Angeline had been born, and her such a bonny and happy child, you'd have thought she was the most gifted and perfect being in all creation. And any parent wants to protect their child, if they're worth their salt. But Philip and Margery's decision to keep the girl in what amounted to a state of seclusion didn't bode well now – or for the future. She was the most innocent of lambs.

Hector Stewart cleared his throat, and George's gaze turned to him. As much as he had liked and respected Philip, he disliked his brother. The man was weak and ineffectual and uppish into the bargain, but he had always held his tongue about Hector, because Philip wouldn't hear a word against him. Which was commendable, he supposed, but sometimes not seeing the flaws in someone you loved could have far-reaching consequences. There were constant rumours at the Gentlemen's Club about Hector's drinking and gambling, and if even half of them were true, the man was on the road to perdition. Eustace Preston had told him only last week that it was common knowledge Hector took himself off to Newcastle these days to certain gambling dens where fortunes were regularly won and lost. Mostly lost, he'd be bound. And this was the individual to whom Philip and Margery had entrusted their beloved daughter.

Hector cleared his throat again even more pointedly, and George put his thoughts behind him and picked up the document in front of him on the desk.

Addressing himself to Angeline, he said gently, 'This is the last will and testament of your parents, child. Do you understand what that means?' When she nodded, he continued, 'I will read it word for word in a moment, but essentially your parents left everything to you, which makes it simple. They appointed your uncle as your guardian, should they die before you reached the age of twenty-one and were unmarried. You will reside with him and have a personal monthly allowance, and your uncle will also have a sum of money each month for as long as you are in his care.'

Angeline stared at the solicitor. 'Leave Oakfield? No, they would never have said that.'

'I'm sorry.' George had been dreading this meeting, and it was being every bit as bad as he'd feared. The girl looked even more bereft than before, if that were possible.

'But why? Why would they want me to leave our home?'

'Angeline, you are fifteen years old.' Hector spoke firmly, but not unkindly. 'You cannot run a home on your own – the very idea is ridiculous. There are bills to pay, daily decisions to make, servants to keep in order, and umpteen other things.'

'The house runs itself under Mrs Lee, my mama always said so, and the servants don't need keeping in order. They . . . they're like family.'

Hector looked askance.

Realizing she'd said the wrong thing, Angeline swallowed hard. 'Miss Robson could take up permanent residence,' she said desperately. 'That way I'm not alone here, am I? She would keep everything and everyone as it should be, and she could report directly to you. And I could still live here.' Turning to the solicitor, she added, 'There's enough money for that, isn't there, Mr Appleby?'

Without giving the solicitor a chance to respond, and with a thread of impatience in his voice, Hector said, 'It's not a question of money, Angeline. Your father stated his wishes very clearly, and what you are suggesting is quite ludicrous. You will come to live with me within the week. That is the end of the matter. My final word. You may bring anything you wish, of course, and Miss Robson has agreed to continue to give you your lessons each morning. This house will be sold forthwith, and the proceeds added to the trust.'

'But Mrs Lee and Cook, and everyone?'

'The servants will be given excellent references and three months' wages in lieu of notice. The senior staff – the housekeeper, cook and butler – will receive six months' wages. This is very generous, believe me.' Her uncle's tone made it clear that if this stipulation hadn't been in the will, his treatment of the servants would have been very different. 'Now, Mr Appleby has pointed out that you will need a personal maid, m'dear. Which is not necessary at present, in my bachelor abode.'

Hector smiled his thin smile, but Angeline was too distraught by the turn of events to respond. Oakfield sold? And the staff dismissed? Just like that? This was their home, too – couldn't he see that?

'Mr Appleby suggested you might wish to bring your current housemaid with you in that capacity.' Hector's sniff of disapproval indicated that he couldn't for the life of him see why. A servant was a servant, after all. Now, if it had been a pet dog or cat . . . 'But I thought a maid already trained in that respect would be more suitable.'

Feeling as though she was drowning, Angeline caught at the lifeline that the kindly solicitor had provided. 'Myrtle attended to Mama when she had need of it,' she said quickly, 'and I would prefer her to a stranger.'

'So be it. Now, Mr Appleby, perhaps you would be so good as to read the will?'

When the solicitor eventually finished speaking, only two things had really registered through Angeline's turmoil. First, that she wouldn't come into her inheritance until she was twenty-one or married – whichever came first. Second, that she was a very rich young woman. This Mr Appleby had impressed upon her, adding that it was why her father had wanted to see to it that she was under her uncle's protection until she was mature enough to cope with such a responsibility.

'Your father has tied the trust up in such a way that no monies – other than your allowance and the stipend paid to your uncle for as long as you reside with him – can be extracted. By you or anyone else.' George Appleby's gaze flicked to Hector for a moment. He wasn't fooled by his blank countenance. Philip's brother had expected a bequest of some kind, although George couldn't see why. Philip had been amazingly generous to Hector when their father had died, setting him up in his own business and buying him a fine house and all. A different man would have been set up for life, but he rather suspected Hector was in trouble, despite his outward facade. Still, he'd make sure Hector didn't get his hands on one penny more than the amount Philip had settled on him each month for Angeline's keep.

Hector stared back at the solicitor. He was aware of George's dislike of him – a feeling he fully reciprocated – and had always resented the high regard in which Philip had held the little man, and the influence the solicitor had had upon his brother. Take this will, for instance. Hector's teeth clenched. He had no doubt Philip had left the mechanics of it to George Appleby, and the solicitor had been instrumental in determining that, even as Angeline's guardian, he couldn't use the trust money. *Cocksure little runt.*

George's eyes returned to Angeline's white face. 'Your father's main concern was to protect you, should the unthinkable happen. You do understand that, don't you?'

Yes, she did, of course she did, but losing Oakfield was almost as bad as the loss of her parents. Her voice unsteady, she whispered, 'Is there no way I can keep the house?'

'I'm sorry, Angeline.'

They looked at each other, and although she felt very small and lost, Angeline held herself straight, her chin lifting. Strangely her mind wasn't in a whirl any longer. Her mama had always said one had to have the grace to accept what couldn't be changed, and the sense to recognize what could. This was the former. Whatever her private feelings on the matter, it was kind of Uncle Hector to take her into his home and offer her protection. Her gaze now going to her uncle, she said quietly, 'I'll try and not be a bother, Uncle.'

'Of course you won't be. We'll get along just fine, m'dear.' It was too hearty, and Hector moderated his tone as he added, 'Your rooms are being prepared and will be ready shortly, so spend the next day or two deciding what you want to bring with you.'

Everything. She wanted to bring everything, because every single stick of furniture, every ornament, every picture, was part of her mother and father. But of course that was impossible. Inclining her head, she said flatly, 'Yes, Uncle.'

It was settled.

Margaret Dickinson

Born in Gainsborough, Lincolnshire, Margaret Dickinson moved to the coast at the age of seven and so began her love for the sea and the Lincolnshire landscape. Her ambition to be a writer began early and she had her first novel published at the age of twenty-five. This was followed by twenty-five further titles including *Plough the Furrow*, *Sow the Seed* and *Reap the Harvest*, which make up her Lincolnshire Fleethaven trilogy. Many of her novels are set in the heart of her home county but in *Tangled Threads* and *Twisted Strands*, the stories include not only Lincolnshire but also the framework knitting and lace industries of Nottingham. Her 2012 and 2013 novels, *Jenny's War* and *The Clippie Girls*, were both top-twenty bestsellers and her 2014 novel, *Fairfield Hall*, went to number nine on the *Sunday Times* bestseller list.

More Books by Margaret Dickinson

Plough the Furrow
Sow the Seed
Reap the Harvest
The Miller's Daughter
Chaff Upon the Wind
The Fisher Lass
The Tulip Girl
The River Folk
Tangled Threads
Twisted Strands
Red Sky in the Morning
Without Sin
Pauper's Gold
Wish Me Luck
Sing As We Go
Suffragette Girl
Sons and Daughters
Forgive and Forget
Jenny's War
The Clippie Girls
Fairfield Hall

FAIRFIELD HALL
by Margaret Dickinson

A matter of honour. A sense of duty. A time for courage.

Ruthlessly ambitious Ambrose Constantine is determined that his daughter, Annabel, shall marry into the nobility. A fish merchant and self-made man, he has only his wealth to buy his way into society.

When Annabel's secret meetings with Gilbert, a young man employed at her father's offices, stop suddenly, she learns that he has mysteriously disappeared. Heartbroken, she finds solace with her grandparents on their Lincolnshire farm, but her father will not allow her to hide herself in the countryside and enlists the help of a business connection to launch his daughter into society.

During the London Season, Annabel is courted by James Lyndon, the Earl of Fairfield, whose country estate is only a few miles from her grandfather's farm.

Believing herself truly loved at last, Annabel accepts his offer of marriage. It is only when she arrives at Fairfield Hall that she realizes the true reason behind James's proposal and the part her scheming father has played.

Throughout the years that follow, Annabel experiences both heartache and joy, and the birth of her son should finally secure the future of the Fairfield Estate. But there are others who lay claim to the inheritance, igniting a feud that will only reach its resolution in the trenches of the First World War.

Read on for an extract from
Fairfield Hall by Margaret Dickinson

Prologue

Tiffany parked the car at the side of the road and climbed the gentle slope of hill towards the grand house at the top. She dared not bring her little car any further, for the day was bleak, the road slippery and she feared losing control of the vehicle. *Beatrice* wasn't good on icy roads, never mind any kind of hill. As the ground flattened out, she paused to catch her breath and look around her. To the west lay the wolds, undulating gently and covered in a frost that had not melted since morning. Directly below, Fairfield village nestled in a shallow vale. The light was fading even though it was still early afternoon and already lights flickered in several of the windows of the cottages lining the one main street. Beyond the village, she could see farms dotted on the hillsides. At one end of the village street stood the church with the vicarage beside it. She could close her eyes and imagine herself back in time; Tiffany doubted that the scene had changed much in the last hundred years, except, of course, for the cars parked on either side of the road – a necessity when the nearest market town was five miles away. And there was now only one village shop that sold everything instead of the butcher, the grocer and so on, who would all once have been able to make a living even in this small community. Now the villagers would head into the nearest town – Thorpe St Michael – to the supermarket for their weekly shopping, using the local village store only for emergencies. Even the smithy-cum-wheelwright's that had once been the heartbeat of a rural community would be long gone, unless, of course, the blacksmith's business had survived by making bespoke fancy wrought-iron work.

She turned to look up again at the house standing sentinel over the village and resumed her walk, shivering a little. March opening times, she'd read in a leaflet about Fairfield Hall, were Sundays and Wednesdays, and today, Mother's Day, it seemed fitting that she should visit.

She was breathing hard by the time she'd walked along the curving driveway, lined with lime trees in their winter nakedness, though she knew they'd be a lovely sight in summer. She paused a moment, before passing beneath an archway into a courtyard. In front of her were stables and to her left, three coach houses. Completing the square were other buildings, which once, she guessed, might have housed the laundry and workshops. In the centre of the courtyard was a magnificent beech tree and, to her right, she could see the side entrance to the house. Nearing it, she saw the notice: Please Use The Front Entrance. Passing through a small gate, she wandered round the corner of the house and climbed the steps. The impressive three-storey square house, with its front door positioned centrally, faced to the west with six windows on the ground floor and seven on the upper storeys. Closer now, she could see that there was also a basement partly below ground level. Attached on the northern side was a lower building – only two storeys high. The smooth lawn in front of the house sloped down towards the village. To the side she could see more gardens and guessed that behind the house there was perhaps a kitchen plot that would have grown produce to help feed the household. Beyond the grounds belonging to the house were cultivated fields where, in summer, there would be ripening corn bordered with bright-headed poppies. She waited for what seemed an age before the door was opened slowly by an elderly man, dressed strangely, she thought, in a morning suit. He looked like a butler stepping out of the pages of a history book. But his wrinkled face beamed and his old eyes twinkled. 'Good afternoon, miss. How nice to see a visitor. Please come in.'

Tiffany stepped into the hall and wiped her feet on the square of thick matting. 'I expect you don't get many in the winter and especially on a day like this.'

The old man chuckled. 'Not many, miss, no.'

To one side of the hall, a log fire burned in a pretty fire-place lined with blue and white Delft tiles and Tiffany, drawn by its warmth, held her cold hands towards it.

'Would you like me to give you a guided tour,' the man asked, 'or would you prefer to wander through the house on your own? It's clearly marked where you're allowed to go, so . . .'

'I'd like the guided tour, please.'

He smiled again. No doubt he was delighted to be needed.

'Whenever you're ready, then, miss. I don't think we'll get any more visitors today, so you have my undivided attention.'

'That's nice,' Tiffany murmured sincerely. 'Thank you.' There was so much she wanted to know about this house and she was sure she'd found the right person to tell her.

'This is the entrance hall, of course,' the guide began and then he led her into the room on the left-hand side of the hall. 'This was once the housekeeper's room so that she could see who was coming up the drive – the family returning home or visitors arriving – and warn the rest of the servants. In the late 1890s it was used as the estate office. Beyond it we have what would have been the drawing room, but in later years, we understand, it became known as the music room. Isn't it magnificent?'

Paintings and portraits lined the oak-panelled walls; in one corner stood a grand piano, in another an oak long-case clock solemnly ticked away the hours as perhaps it had done for over two hundred and fifty years.

He led her out of another door and along a corridor. 'Those rooms are just a modern kitchen and sitting room and this,' he said as they passed a staircase on the right-hand side, 'is what the servants would use, but *this*,' he emphasized as they passed once more through the entrance hall and to the southern end of the house, 'is the main staircase.' The walls above the oak staircase were again lined with family portraits. There was such a history to this house. Tiffany's heart beat a little faster.

'We'll go upstairs in a moment,' her guide said, 'but first let me show you the library here to the right of the stairs . . .' The room – as she had imagined it would be – was lined with shelves of books. 'And then this room to the left is what used to be the morning room. It faces to the east at the back of the house so it always gets the morning sun. Sadly,' he smiled at her, 'we haven't any today.

'Now, upstairs we have the family's private sitting room and straight opposite are the best bedrooms. Further along, you will see that the living-in servants also had bedrooms on this floor.'

'Really?' Tiffany laughed. 'I thought servants were always confined to the attics?'

'Not in this house, miss.' He smiled. 'The top floor has the nursery and probably a room for a nursery nurse or governess and also a couple of very nice guest bedrooms.'

I wonder where she slept? Tiffany thought as they retraced their steps downstairs. *I'd like to think that I've been standing in her bedroom.*

He showed her the huge kitchen in the basement and other, smaller rooms that were used for different purposes: a wine cellar, a game larder, a still room and the butler's pantry. He even showed her the row of fourteen bells, which summoned the servants.

'And now I'll take you back to my favourite room in the house. I've deliberately left it until last.'

When they entered the dining room, where portraits of the more recent family members were hanging, Tiffany's interest sharpened.

'The main part of the house was built in the early 1700s by the Lyndon family in the style of Sir Christopher Wren, and the two-storey extension to the north was added much later,' the guide told her. 'It's strange to find such a house as this in the countryside, isn't it? It's more suited to a town house.'

Tiffany said nothing, willing him to go on with the stories of the family. That was what interested her.

'The hereditary title, the Earl of Fairfield, was granted to Montague Lyndon at the end of a distinguished military career in 1815 and thereafter each generation sent a son into the Army, usually the second son, if there was one, so that the title was safeguarded. The eldest son always inherited the title and he was expected to run the estate.' They moved on slowly down the line of portraits, the guide pointing briefly to each one. 'That's the second earl, the third, the fourth and the fifth, and now we come to the sixth Earl of Fairfield, James Lyndon.'

Tiffany gazed up at the full-length portrait of a man in military uniform. He was tall with brown hair and dark brown eyes that, strangely, seemed to stare coldly down at her. There was no smile, no warmth in his face.

'As you can see,' her guide said, 'James was a soldier, too, and, by all accounts, a very good one. He was the second son and should never have inherited the title but his elder brother, Albert, died young.'

Tiffany took a step forward and then stopped, her gaze held by the picture of a young woman hanging on the opposite side of the fireplace to the one of the sixth earl. Her hair was as black as a raven's feathers. She had dark violet eyes and flawless skin. She was dressed in a blue satin gown with a necklace around her graceful neck. Tiffany hoped the artist had painted a true representation of her.

She bit her lip, hardly daring to ask. 'Who is this?'

'Ah, now that is Lady Annabel, James's wife. Isn't

she lovely?' They stood a moment in silence, in awe of the woman's striking beauty. In answer to Tiffany's unspoken question, he added, 'And she was every bit as lovely as her portrait.'

Tiffany glanced at him. To the twenty-year-old girl, her guide looked ancient, but even he couldn't be old enough to remember Lady Annabel, could he? But it seemed he was.

He smiled. 'My grandfather worked here as a gardener and he used to talk about her. In fact, you couldn't get him to stop talking about her. I only saw her twice and she was getting on a bit by then, of course, but she was still striking. And everyone loved her, except,' he sighed heavily, 'the one person who should have loved her the most. Poor lady.'

'Tell me about her – please.' Tiffany couldn't help the pleading tone in her voice and, sensing it, the man smiled down at her.

'It's a long story.'

'I'm in no rush. It's – it's what I came for. I'd love to learn as much as I can about her, but only if you've time.'

'Oh, I've time. But let's sit down, my dear. My old legs aren't what they used to be.'

They sat down on two chairs near the fire, but facing the two portraits.

'Well, now, where to begin?' He fell silent for a moment, his gaze still on the enchanting face in the painting, and then he murmured again, 'Where to begin?'

One

'Please can we go home, Miss Annabel? It's freezing.'

'Just another five minutes,' Annabel murmured, staring through the gloom of the winter's evening, watching the road ahead.

They were sitting in the horse-drawn chaise on the seafront at Cleethorpes, not far from the pier that stretched out into the cold sea. There were no holidaymakers today, no visitors walking its length. Although the chaise offered a little more shelter than an open trap, the wind blew in from the sea, stinging their faces and chilling their bones.

'If you're late for dinner, your father will ask questions. And you know I can't tell lies. I go bright red and he knows straightaway.'

'I don't expect you to tell lies for me, Jane.'

The maid shivered. 'The horse is getting cold too. See how he's pawing at the ground.'

The chaise rocked dangerously as the restless horse moved.

'Miss Annabel,' Jane said firmly, 'he's not coming and we're both going to be in such trouble when we get back. What will Mrs Rowley say if I'm not there to help with the dinner? You know I have to help out in the kitchen.'

The Constantine household had few staff: a butler, Roland Walmsley, who also served as valet to his master, a cook-cum-housekeeper, Mrs Rowley, a kitchen maid, Lucy, and Jane, who was everything else; house-maid and lady's maid to Mrs Constantine and to Miss Annabel. The only outside staff were a part-time gardener and a groom, Billy, who looked after the two horses and usually drove Annabel or her mother wherever they wanted to go. But today, Annabel had insisted upon driving the chaise herself with only her maid for company.

Annabel sighed and took up the reins, saying, 'Gee up.' The horse, glad of some activity at last, lurched forward and the two girls clutched at the sides of the vehicle.

'He'll have us over,' Jane muttered, but the sure-footed horse began to trot happily towards home. A little way along the road into Grimsby, Annabel pulled on the reins so that the horse turned to the right. Prince hesitated, yet he obeyed his mistress's instructions.

'Where are you going, miss? This isn't the way home.'

'Isn't it?' Annabel's tone was airy. 'I thought it was. Oh dear, we're lost.' She flicked the reins so that the horse picked up speed, taking them even further away from the road they needed to be on.

'Miss Annabel—'

'I think it's a short cut.'

'No, it isn't. You know very well it isn't. You're going towards the docks,' Jane said, 'and if you've some madcap notion of trying to find him, then – then . . .'

Annabel pulled gently on the reins bringing Prince to a steady walking pace. They reached a crossroads and, skilfully, Annabel turned the horse so that they were facing back the way they had just come. Prince began to trot again, more hopeful now that they were really going home to his warm stable. His speed quickened even more when he recognized Bargate, the road where the Constantines lived.

The house was a square building with a central front door and a bay window on either side. It had a small front garden but a larger one behind the house where their gardener cultivated both flower borders and a kitchen garden. As a young girl, Annabel had been allowed to help in the grounds and in the greenhouse, but as she'd grown older, her father had dictated that she should apply herself to more ladylike occupations.

'It is not fitting for you to be grubbing about in the dirt with only a servant as a companion.'

And so Annabel's love of the land was only satisfied

on her visits to her grandparents who, unbeknown to her father, allowed her to help about the farm.

'There's Billy waiting for us,' Jane said as the chaise came to a halt. She climbed down and then turned to help her young mistress alight, whilst Billy hurried to hold the horse's head.

'Good evening, Billy,' Annabel said with a forced gaiety she was no longer feeling. 'I'm so sorry we're late. We got lost.'

Beside her, she heard Jane pull in a sharp breath but her maid said nothing. Annabel knew the girl would follow her lead and realize that her mistress had given her a ready-made excuse should she be questioned.

'You go in the back way, Jane. I'll go to the front door. Mr Walmsley will let me in. And remember' – she lowered her voice as Billy began to unhitch the horse from the shafts – 'we got lost.'

'Yes, miss.' Jane bobbed a quick curtsy and scurried in through the back door.

Annabel walked around the side of the house and rang the front door bell.

'Good evening, Mr Walmsley,' she said smoothly when the butler opened the door.

Despite having been told to do so on numerous occasions, Annabel flatly refused to address their servants by anything other than their full name or, for the younger ones, their Christian name. She abhorred the use of mere surnames and the butler had long ago given up trying to get her to change. Even her disciplinarian father couldn't enforce the rule with his wayward daughter.

Hearing her voice, Ambrose flung open the door to his study and strode into the hall. He was a short, portly man in his early fifties with a florid complexion and bristling sideburns.

'Where've you been?' he barked.

Annabel turned towards him as she removed her cape, hat and gloves and handed them to Roland Walmsley.

'Out for a drive in the chaise, Father, but I took a wrong turning in the dusk and I got a little lost. I'm so sorry I'm late for dinner.' She turned back to the butler. 'Mr Walmsley, please tell Mrs Rowley that it's my fault Jane is late, not hers.'

Roland Walmsley bowed and hid his smile. He could guess where his young mistress had been, though wild horses would not drag it out of him, nor would he question Jane. She was utterly loyal to Miss Annabel, as were all the servants.

Ambrose glared at his daughter. 'We've held dinner back for half an hour and Mrs Rowley is *not* best pleased.' Mrs Rowley was the only person who warranted – in Ambrose's opinion – a courtesy title. 'You'd better get changed – and be quick about it.'

'Yes, Father.' Annabel bowed her head meekly and

hurried towards the staircase. Ambrose watched her go, his eyes narrowing. Had his ruse worked? he wondered. Annabel's expression gave nothing away. As he watched her climb the stairs, he fancied he saw her shoulders drooping in disappointment. But he couldn't be sure. His daughter was difficult to read. He'd interrogate the maid, he decided. She'd give herself away at once.

But this time, even Jane's resolve proved difficult to break. After dinner was over, he called her to his study. She faced her master fearlessly with wide, innocent eyes. Pulling herself up to her full five feet two inches, she straightened her shoulders and explained calmly, 'We got lost, sir. Miss Annabel took a wrong turning in the dark and then it was difficult to turn the horse round. By the time we got to the right road again, sir, oh, I reckon half an hour or more had gone by.'

Ambrose frowned. 'Did you meet anyone, girl?'

Her eyes widened even more. 'Meet anyone, sir?'

'Don't act stupid with me, girl. You know very well what I mean. Did Miss Annabel have an assignation?'

The girl shook her head vehemently. 'Oh no, sir. We didn't meet anyone.'

Ambrose stepped close to her so that his bulbous red nose was only inches from her small, well-shaped nose. In a low, threatening tone he said slowly, 'If I find out you've been lying to me, girl, it'll be the worse for you. You understand?'

Jane nodded vigorously. 'I wouldn't lie to you, sir. Honest, I wouldn't.'

Ambrose grunted as he stepped away. He still didn't believe her. In his experience anyone who used the word 'honest' to emphasize whatever they were saying, was usually lying.

Jane scuttled back to the kitchen, her cheeks flaming. She hoped that was the last questioning she would have to face from the master, but there was always the mistress to contend with. She was almost more fearsome than Mr Constantine.

'*Now* what have you been up to?' Mrs Rowley frowned. 'Are you in trouble? Because if you are, I want to know about it.'

Oh no, not you an' all! Jane thought. 'Nothing, Mrs Rowley,' she said aloud. 'I was out with Miss Annabel and we were late back. That's all.'

'Oh aye.' Even Mrs Rowley's tone was sceptical. 'And where were you "out", might I ask?'

No, you may not ask, Jane wanted to reply, but she knew that any cheeky retort would earn her a severe reprimand. Instead, she said calmly, 'Just out for a drive, Mrs Rowley. Miss Annabel took a wrong turning in the dark.'

'She shouldn't be out in the dark on her own.'

'She wasn't on her own. I was with her.'

Mrs Rowley rolled her eyes. 'And a fat lot of good you'd have been if there'd been any trouble.'

'What sort of trouble, Mrs Rowley?'

The cook said no more on the subject, contenting herself with a glare and a sharp, 'Get on with your work now you are here. There's a pile of washing-up to be done and Lucy's already drooping with tiredness having to do your work as well as her own while you go off gallivanting.'

For the next few hours there was no time to think, but later that night as she lay in her narrow bed in the attic room she shared with Lucy, Jane thought over the problem she faced with her young mistress. She was devoted to Miss Annabel and would do anything for her – anything – but she was very afraid that what they had been doing over the past few weeks and months was about to be discovered.

Two

Annabel, too, was lying awake.

Why hadn't Gil come to meet her? Was it all over? Didn't he love her any more? Had all his ardent declarations been false?

She had first met Gilbert Radcliffe on a tour of her father's business offices near the fish docks. That day, Gilbert, as the office under-manager, had been deputed to show the boss's daughter around. At only twenty-five he held a surprisingly high position within the company and was well thought of by his immediate superior, the office manager, Mr Smeeton, and her father too. But Annabel was under no illusion that should their secret meetings over the weeks since then be discovered, the young man would no longer be held in such high esteem. Ambrose had big plans for his daughter and they did not include marriage to one of his employees.

Ambrose Constantine was a self-made man. He had been born in one of the poorer areas of the town, the third son of a deckhand on trawlers. He, too, had begun his working life at sea as a deckie-learner, but Ambrose was ambitious. He soon worked his way up to the position of Mate, working hard and enduring the vicious conditions of life at sea to earn good money and save every penny he could. Oh, how he saved his money. But by the time he was twenty, his father and two older brothers had been lost at sea. Broken-hearted, his mother died the following year, leaving Ambrose alone, though the loss of his family only hardened his determination to succeed. He left the sea and became a fish merchant and by the age of twenty-four was employing ten men in the fish docks. He first saw Sarah Armstrong across the aisle of a church, when they were both attending a funeral in late May 1874. She was no beauty, but she was tall and walked with a haughty grace that appealed to Ambrose. She had a strong face and a determined set to her chin. At the gathering in a nearby hotel after the service, Ambrose contrived an introduction to her and found himself gazing into her dark blue eyes and wanting to know all about her.

'How do you know Mr Wheeler?' he began, referring to the deceased, whose coffin they had just watched being lowered ceremoniously into the earth.

'I didn't know him well, but I've accompanied my father today. He used to do business with him and felt he should pay his respects.'

'So – is your father in the fish trade?'

Sarah had laughed. 'No, no, he's a farmer, but he met

Mr Wheeler on market days.' Abraham Wheeler had been an auctioneer throughout Lincolnshire, conducting sales of anything from fish to sheep and cows.

Curious about the fair-haired, stocky young man who, she knew, had deliberately sought an introduction to her, Sarah asked, 'And you? How do you know him?'

'The fish markets.' He smiled. 'He was very helpful to me when I started out.'

'And where have you finished up?'

'Oh, I haven't finished yet, not by a long way.'

Sarah's eyes gleamed as she heard the fire of ambition in his tone. She liked that. She had always bemoaned the fact that she'd been born a girl; men could do so much more with their lives than women, who seemed destined to be wives and mothers and housekeepers. Her father's farm would one day be hers – she was an only child – yet she had no interest in the land. Every summer brought her hayfever misery and even getting too close to a horse could set her sneezing. Each June she spent time near the sea, which seemed to ease her symptoms.

Crossing her fingers at the lie she was about to tell, she said boldly, 'I'm coming to stay in Cleethorpes next week.' She paused, knowing instinctively that he would suggest a meeting. And he did.

Their romance – if it could be called that – progressed swiftly, much to Sarah's parents' dismay. It was more a meeting of like minds, of shared ambition, than a passionate love affair.

'I don't like it,' Edward Armstrong said to his wife, Martha. 'And I don't like *him*. But what can I do? I've talked to her, pleaded with her, even raged at her, but she's set on marrying the fellow. She's twenty-one next month and I suppose if they're really in love . . .'

Martha had put her arms around her husband and laid her dark head against his chest. 'Is it because of the farm, my dear?'

'Only partly. I wanted to pass it down the generations.'

As she heard the heavy sigh deep in his chest, Martha had raised her head and said, with a twinkle in her violet eyes: 'Never mind, perhaps Sarah will give you a grandson who will one day take over Meadow View Farm.'

But Sarah had only given them a granddaughter, Annabel, and it was on her that Edward now pinned all his hopes. He had never agreed with the belief that genteel young ladies should spend their time drawing, painting, sewing and playing the piano. Instead, he had instructed his daughter, Sarah, in the basic rudiments of accountancy and had introduced her to the precarious delights of buying and selling shares. At the time, he could not have foreseen that her quick mind and intuitive head for business, together with all that he had taught her, would equip Sarah not for running the farm as he had hoped but for helping her husband run his growing business.

Grudgingly, Edward was forced to admit that Ambrose was a clever and successful man. In 1883, Ambrose had been the first owner of a steam trawler and by the time Annabel reached adulthood, he was the biggest steam trawler owner in the Grimsby docks. Seeing that Sarah was well provided for by her prosperous husband, Edward made his will in favour of his granddaughter, leaving his five-hundred-acre farm in the Lincolnshire wolds to her. One day it would all belong to Annabel, but for the moment, Edward and his wife remained in good health and continued to run Meadow View Farm themselves. And on her frequent visits, Edward delighted in the young girl's intelligence and her capacity for learning quickly. He was heartened that she seemed to possess nothing of the ruthless ambition of her father and – it had to be said – of her mother. She soon knew all the farmhands by their first names and, as a youngster, played with their children. But it was when riding on horseback around the fields with her grandfather that Annabel's face shone and she chattered with a multitude of questions. In turn, Edward was thrilled by the girl's enthusiasm and growing love for the land. His farm would be in safe hands and he began to teach Annabel, too, the rudiments of bookkeeping and the ups and downs of the stock market. He introduced her to the stockbroker he used in Thorpe St Michael, Henry Parker, and together the two men guided and schooled the young girl until she was old enough to deal for herself.

What Edward didn't know – and for a long time neither did Ambrose – was that it was on these journeys to visit her grandparents that Annabel and Gilbert Radcliffe began to meet. Only Jane knew and now the burden of knowledge was too great for the young maid to endure. But she need not have worried that she would be questioned or even blamed; word had already reached Ambrose from his office manager, who had heard the gossip and noticed that his young protégé's absences from work coincided with Miss Annabel's visits to her grandparents.

Ambrose had acted swiftly.

'Father, I'd like to pay a visit to the docks. It's quite some time since my last visit,' Annabel said at breakfast the following morning.

Ambrose was a familiar sight on the dockside in his dark suit and bowler hat inspecting the most recent catches laid out neatly in containers. Annabel loved The Pontoon, the covered fish market where the early morning catches were auctioned. Whenever Ambrose could be persuaded to take her with him, she stood quietly watching and marvelling at the speed of the auctioneer conducting sale after sale. He seemed to know what each of his customers would want. But, much to Annabel's disappointment as she grew older, Ambrose forbade her to go so often. He didn't like to see the fishermen eying his lovely daughter. The docks, he decreed, were no place for a lady.

'But I'm not a lady,' Annabel had argued futilely.

'Ah, but one day you will be,' had been her father's only reply.

'Of course, my dear,' Ambrose agreed smoothly now. 'What would you like to see? The ships? The fish docks? Of course, the herring girls aren't here for some months yet. I know you like to watch them, but—'

'Your offices, Father. I'd like to visit your offices.'

'Then you may come with me this morning.'

'That won't be necessary. I can make my own way there.'

'No need,' he replied, deliberately keeping his tone mild. 'I should like you to drive with me.'

Annabel had no choice but to bow her head in acquiescence.

Ambrose wanted to shout at her, to roar his disapproval of her actions, but he knew it was not the way to deal with his strong-willed daughter. The path he had chosen was far better and was already bearing fruit, if his suspicions regarding the previous evening's escapade were correct. Instead of causing a confrontation, he smiled across the table at her. 'It pleases me that you should take an interest in the business. I thought you were all set to become a farmer.' They all knew the terms of Edward's will.

Ambrose's tone sobered as he said warningly, 'One day you will be a very wealthy woman. Not only will you inherit your grandfather's farm, but also my company. You do understand that, don't you?'

Annabel smiled. 'But not for many years yet, I hope, Father.'

'I hope not, but your grandparents are both in their sixties. Just remember that. And now' – he rose from the table – 'I have a little paperwork to do, but I'll be ready to leave in about an hour.'

Ambrose closed the door of his study and went to stand before the window looking out on to the garden behind the house. He was pensive for a few moments before sitting down at his desk, picking up his pen and beginning to write a letter.

Dear Lord Fairfield . . .

When they arrived at her father's offices, not far from where the dock tower stood guardian over the forest of masts and funnels as the trawlers jostled for position to unload their catches, Annabel hurried to the manager's office. She knew that Gilbert occupied a desk in the same room. Ambrose followed his daughter at a more leisurely pace, deliberately allowing her to go ahead of him. A small smile played on his lips. In the outer office sat a middle-aged man at a desk and in the corner a young woman tapped at a typewriter.

'Good morning,' Annabel greeted them both and

then turned to the older man. 'Is G— Mr Radcliffe in?'

The man blinked, but before he could answer, the door to the inner office was flung open and Mr Smeeton, the manager, appeared.

'Ah, Miss Constantine, please come in. Is your father with you?'

'Yes, he's coming.'

She moved quickly into his office and glanced around. There was no sign of Gilbert. Neither was there any sign of his desk on the far side of the room where it had once stood.

'Please sit down,' Mr Smeeton said kindly. 'Would you like some tea?'

'No, no, thank you. Mr Smeeton—?' she began urgently, but her question was interrupted by the sound of voices in the outer office. The door opened again and her father entered the room. Annabel cast a beseeching glance at Mr Smeeton, but said no more.

'Good morning, Smeeton.'

'Sir.' Mr Smeeton gave a tiny deferential bow towards his employer and moved a chair for him to sit down.

Ambrose looked about him and asked casually, 'No Radcliffe this morning?'

'No, sir. He – um – he's left.'

A startled gasp escaped Annabel, but with amazing self-control she bit back her question. Instead, it was

Ambrose who raised his eyebrows and said, 'Really? That was rather sudden, wasn't it?'

'Very sudden, sir. He didn't even stay to work out his notice.'

'How come?' Ambrose asked quite calmly, laying his hat and cane on Mr Smeeton's desk and pulling off his gloves whilst Annabel watched and listened with growing alarm. She gripped the arms of the chair and bit down hard on her lower lip.

'It seems,' Mr Smeeton went on, 'that he came into a sum of money very unexpectedly and he's – um – used it to emigrate to America, I believe.'

'Emigrate?' Annabel gasped, no longer able to keep silent. Nor could she stop the colour rising in her face. Gilbert gone? Without a word to her? 'For how long?'

Mr Smeeton avoided meeting her gaze. 'I presume for good, Miss Constantine.'

'But what about—?' she began, but managed to stop the words just in time. Instead, she finished rather lamely, 'his family?'

'I don't think he has much in the way of family. His parents are dead. He has one brother, I believe . . .'

Out of the corner of her eye, she saw her father frown and Mr Smeeton added hastily, 'But I don't even know where he lives. I understand they never saw much of each other.'

Annabel dared not say more, dared not ask any more

questions – not in front of her father. But somehow, some time, she would interrogate Mr Smeeton further.

'Now, my dear,' Ambrose said smoothly, 'you said you wanted to look around the docks.'

'Of course, Father,' she said meekly and rose, though she found her legs were trembling. She felt faint with shock. Gilbert had gone, had left her without a word.

'Are you all right Miss Constantine?' Mr Smeeton asked gently, with genuine concern. He had noticed how the girl had flushed on hearing the news about Gilbert Radcliffe, but now she had turned very pale.

Annabel lifted her chin. 'I am perfectly well, thank you, Mr Smeeton. Now, Father, where shall we begin?'

Annie Murray

Annie Murray was born in Berkshire and read English at St John's College, Oxford. Her first 'Birmingham' novel, *Birmingham Rose*, hit *The Times* bestseller list when it was published in 1995. Annie Murray has four children and lives in Reading.

More Books by Annie Murray

Birmingham Rose
Birmingham Friends
Birmingham Blitz
Orphan of Angel Street
Poppy Day
The Narrowboat Girl
Chocolate Girls
Water Gypsies
Miss Purdy's Class
Family of Women
Where Earth Meets Sky
The Bells of Bournville Green
A Hopscotch Summer
Soldier Girl
All the Days of Our Lives
My Daughter, My Mother
The Women of Lilac Street
Meet Me Under the Clock

MEET ME UNDER THE CLOCK
by Annie Murray

Growing up in Birmingham, Sylvia and Audrey White-house have always been like chalk and cheese. When the Second World War breaks out, Sylvia is still dreaming of her forthcoming marriage to fiancé Ian while Audrey jumps at the career opportunities the WAAF throws her way.

Audrey joins the ranks at RAF Cardington but soon finds that her new freedom also brings temptation. When she goes too far, the consequences ripple through the Whitehouse family. Meanwhile, Sylvia is doing her bit as a railway porter, much to Ian's dismay. Ian thinks the job is unfeminine – unlike Sylvia's new friend Kitty, who is as sweet and pretty as can be. But Kitty's innocent nature hides a dark secret . . .

As the pressures of rationing, bombing raids and sleepless nights grow, the two sisters must decide what they really want from life and whether they're brave enough to fight for it.

Read on for an extract from *Meet Me Under the Clock*
by Annie Murray

1940

One

Sylvia was helping her mother with the weekly wash when she heard it. She was standing at the kitchen table, hands in a bowl of soapy water, while Mom was feeding clothes through the mangle. Sylvia pushed some dark curls of hair away from her forehead with her arm and tilted her head.

'Ssh, listen – what's that?'

Her mother, Pauline Whitehouse, her thick red hair held back in a flowery turban, stilled the handle of the mangle. They could both hear it then, coming from next door's garden.

'Oh good Lord, it sounds like Marjorie!' Pauline rushed for the back door, wiping her hands on her apron.

It was raining outside. Over the pattering drops Sylvia could clearly hear the sounds of distress. Her heart pounded. Surely those noises weren't coming from cheerful, good-natured Mrs Gould? But already she knew, with a terrible dread: something had happened to one of the boys.

In the distance she heard her mother's soothing tones and Marjorie Gould's choking cries. Mom led Marjorie through the gap dividing the two gardens and towards the house. Sylvia forced herself to move. She rushed to wipe her hands and put the kettle on.

'Come on, bab, let's get you in the dry,' Pauline was saying. 'That's it, let's sit you down . . .'

There were dark spots of rain on Mom's apron and on Marjorie's dress, which was royal blue, patterned with little white anchors. Sylvia froze again with shock. She had known Marjorie Gould all her life – Marjorie was like a second mother to her – and she had never, ever seen her like this before. Marjorie was a big-boned, normally splendid-looking woman with thick, blonde hair, who favoured bright frocks and lipstick. But today she was hunched over, shaking and weeping, her face contorted. As Mom guided her to the chair by the unlit range, Sylvia saw that Marjorie had no shoes on. She had run out into the wet in her stockinged feet.

'No!' she was sobbing. 'No . . . No . . . !' There was a piece of paper crumpled tightly in her right hand.

'Get the kettle on, Sylv,' Pauline said.

'I already have.' Her eyes met her mother's and Pauline caught hold of Sylvia's arm and pulled her hurriedly down the hall, out of earshot.

'It's Raymond.' They were standing by the coat hooks. An old black mac of Dad's sagged from a peg. 'He's . . . Oh good heavens—' Sylvia saw the awful truth of it hit her mother. Her hands came up to her cheeks. 'His ship's gone down.'

'No!' Sylvia gasped. Raymond was the oldest of Marjorie Gould's three sons: Raymond, Laurie and Paul. 'But does that mean . . . ? Is he . . . ?'

Pauline looked down with a faint nod. 'Must be.'

Sylvia felt sick and shaky, even though her mind could not fully take in the news. Raymond, the boy next door. Raymond, a gentle, dark-haired lad who had gone off and joined the Navy, looking for a new life, a way to escape from his father and to separate himself from the girl he loved, but who did not love him back – Audrey, Sylvia's elder sister.

'If only Laurie hadn't just joined up as well,' Pauline said, anguished. Laurie had not long gone into the RAF. 'This *terrible,* wicked war . . .' She squeezed Sylvia's arm. 'I must go back to her.'

Sylvia sank down onto the stairs as her mother headed back to the kitchen. She heard Mrs Gould break into more gulping sobs. Crouching on the third step up, she gripped her hands together to try and stop them trembling. She had to remind herself to breathe. Raymond – Raymond Gould, aged twenty-one. Sweet, solemn Raymond, just a year older than herself, whom she had known for as long as she could remember. Raymond, who would now never be twenty-two, or -three or -four.

She rested her head in her hands, staring, unseeing, at the tiled hall floor.

Raymond was in so many of the family photographs.

Sylvia moved restlessly around the house that afternoon. Mom was next door with Mrs Gould and her youngest son Paul. Dad and Audrey were at work and her brother Jack was at school. Sylvia worked evenings, but it was her day off. She found herself wandering into the front room. They did not light the fire in there very often and the atmosphere was rather cold and stiff compared with the back room, where they all ate every night around the table.

There were three dark-green chairs arranged round the fire with its polished brass fender. On a side-table facing the window Mom kept her carefully dusted collection of framed photographs, arranged on a red chenille cloth. Sylvia and Audrey as little girls smiled out of the most eye-catching one. At least, Sylvia was smiling. She had been six when the picture was taken and Audrey eight. Sylvia, pink-cheeked, with her cloud of black, frizzy hair, was beaming amiably, displaying a

selection of teeth and gaps. Audrey looked more solemn, unwilling to smile if she did not feel like it. She did
have a full row of teeth, though.

Sylvia always wondered why Mom had gone to the
trouble of having her children's pictures done just
when they had half their teeth missing. The one of their
younger brother Jack, freckly and auburn-haired like
Mom, showed him grinning, with black gaps along his
gums. There was Mom and Dad's wedding photograph: Dad skinny and happy, Mom with her hair piled
magnificently on her head and looking shy. And in the
front row there were tiny portraits in ornate pewter
frames of each of the three of them as babies, once they
could sit up. As they grew older there were lots of
pictures, because the two dads, Ted Whitehouse and
Stanley Gould, had bought a Beau Brownie camera
between them. From all of these photographs the
Gould boys smiled out as well. Raymond was in so
many of them, dark-eyed and serious, while Laurie
was blond like his mother. Paul came along later.

Sylvia chose a picture with all of them in, and sat
down to study it. Raymond, about nine in the picture,
was standing at the end of the line of children in the
back garden where they'd spent so many hours playing. The picture seemed so real and close. She could
hear his piping boy's voice, before it broke into a deep,
manly one; and she remembered his skinny legs in

baggy shorts, tearing along the garden. Raymond bowling a tennis ball for cricket games, furious when Audrey whacked it over onto the railway line. Raymond intent on his homework, getting more and more nervy as he floundered at the grammar school into which Stanley, his father, had steamrollered him.

She looked closely into Raymond's eyes. He was so familiar, like a brother. She realized then, though, with a pang, that in her whole life she had scarcely ever been alone with Raymond or talked to him on her own. They had always been in a gang. He had just been one of those things she took for granted, like the furniture, or the buses in Kings Heath High Street, or the Market Hall in Birmingham. And now Raymond was gone and the Market Hall had been wrecked by a bombing raid.

All through the long 'phoney war' of last winter Raymond had been on HMS *Esk*, a destroyer, laying mines around the coast of Norway and Holland. The ship had taken part in the evacuation of troops from Dunkirk. Sylvia knew all this must have made Stanley Gould prouder than he would ever be capable of saying. The last time Raymond came home on leave he had been just as serious, but he looked older, and strong and capable. Sylvia had wondered then whether Audrey might change her mind and love Raymond back. She knew Marjorie was hoping – and Mom. But no. Poor Raymond carried his flame for Audrey quietly and stoically. And now . . .

'Oh, Raymond,' she said, smoothing her finger over the glass. How could it be that he was dead, that they would never see him again, ever? Cradling the photograph in her arms, she rocked back and forth as if giving comfort to Raymond and to herself. Gradually the ache in her released into sobs and the tears came.

It was all they could think about.

Ted Whitehouse, Sylvia's dad, was a foreman at the Rover in Acocks Green. It was one of Herbert Austin's shadow factories, set up before the war to disguise the whereabouts of armaments production by removing some of it from well-known factory sites. The works were making parts for Bristol Hercules engines.

Since the bombing started Ted had to take his turn at the works, on fire-watch, but it was not his shift tonight. He was able to go round and commiserate with Stanley. Ted, a tall, slender man with dark hair and eyes, looked pale and strained after this experience. He sat down in the kitchen to unlace his boots. Sylvia and Jack, who was twelve, were in there with Pauline already. Pauline had broken the news to Jack when he came in from school. He went up to his room for a bit and now he was silent and withdrawn.

'This is when you really know you're at war,' Ted

said, pushing each boot off with the other foot.

'Oh, I think we all know that, love,' his wife said. They had got used to so many things already in this war: gas masks, the shortages, the dark streets and blacked-out houses, the terrible news as the Germans invaded one country after another. But this was the worst so far. This brought the war right up close, into their homes and hearts. Pauline's eyes were red. 'How's Stanley?' she asked.

Ted shook his head, laying the black boots side-by-side. 'As you'd expect.'

They heard the front door open as Audrey came in and they all exchanged looks.

Ted got up. 'You tell her,' he said quietly, moving out of the kitchen, boots in hand. 'I've had all I can stand.'

They heard him say, 'All right, love?' quietly as he passed Audrey. She came into the kitchen in her office clothes: a dark-blue skirt and white blouse. She worked, without enthusiasm, as a shorthand typist for an insurance company. Crossing the kitchen, she flung herself into the chair next to the range in which Marjorie Gould had howled out her grief earlier.

Audrey was tall and slender, very much like her father with her brown eyes, dark lashes and long, sleek hair, which was pinned back in a fashionable style for work. Though less obviously pretty and pink-cheeked than Sylvia, she had a striking, strong-featured face and a large, well-defined nose. She gave off a fiery kind of energy, which attracted people to her. Among the three children in the family, she was definitely always the boss.

She slid her black court shoes off, crossed one leg over, twitching her foot impatiently up and down. She looked round at everyone.

'What's the matter with you lot?' she asked. 'You've got faces as long as Livery Street.'

In the silence that followed she uncrossed her legs and sat up, really taking in that something was amiss.

'Why are you all in here?' It was rare for Jack to be in the kitchen at this time, as the grammar school gave him so much homework.

Sylvia and her mother looked at each other.

'Audrey, love,' Pauline said, slowly, as if she didn't want to bring the words out. 'There's been some terrible news today.'

Jack made a small sound, as if stifling a sob, and covered his face with his hands. Sylvia felt her chest tighten so that she could hardly breathe.

Audrey's eyes searched their mother's face. 'News? How d'you mean?'

Pauline explained. Sylvia watched Audrey's face as she tried to make sense of what her mother was saying. Her eyes widened. She curled forward, arms crossed, hugging herself.

'Could he be alive?' She just managed to keep her voice steady. 'He could be . . . I mean, he can swim, can't he?'

'I think it's over,' Pauline said gently. 'There was a telegram from the Navy.'

'Marjorie came in earlier,' Sylvia said. 'She was in a very bad state.'

Pauline went to Audrey to put her arm round her. 'Audrey, bab . . . ?' But at the first touch on her shoulder, Audrey threw her mother off and got up.

'That's terrible news,' she said. 'Poor Mr and Mrs Gould.' She wasn't meeting any of their eyes. 'I can't really take it in. I'm going up to take my things off.'

She walked out of the kitchen, leaving them all watching the space she had left. Her shoes were discarded at untidy angles next to the range.

'Oh dear, oh dear,' Pauline said. She sank down on one of the chairs, looking completely exhausted.

Two

The Whitehouses and the Goulds had lived side by side in Kings Heath in their quiet, terraced neighbourhood for years. First Pauline and Ted moved into their house, with Audrey as a baby. When the house next door came up for rent a few months later, the Goulds moved in when they had just had Raymond.

The children grew up together and rubbed along, as youngsters are expected to, and most of the time it was lovely. But there were always things that were not so nice, that stayed with you – like that one afternoon Sylvia would never forget.

Mr Gould made them all play one of his games. Stanley Gould was forever thinking up pastimes designed to make his sons count or add up. Dad said that Stanley had always been 'a clever bugger', and he pushed his sons into anything he thought would make them grow up to be brilliant engineers. He loved anything to do with counting. One of his favourite hobbies was collecting loco numbers. They often saw him craning over the fence at the Kings and Castles and the other engines rushing along the LMS line. Just beyond the iron railings that bordered their gardens was the cutting, its vegetation scorched by fires from the scattering sparks.

Stanley Gould was a short, restless man, his hair brushed back over his head like two tarry bird's wings. He had a clipped black moustache and, at the left side of his mouth, a metal tooth, which glistened when he spoke. Sylvia found it fascinating. Stanley worked as pattern-maker in a firm that, for the war effort, had gone over to making parts for tanks. He was quick-minded, competent and chirpy and expected everyone else to be the same. On this particular warm summer afternoon, when the children were playing in the Goulds' garden, he started giving orders.

'Come on,' he urged. Sylvia could sense his impatience underneath the jolly tone. Life was for getting on – it was no good idling about, wasting time! She felt a plunge of nervousness in her stomach. 'Line up now, in age order. Raymond first.'

Audrey was never easy to order around at the best of times. She planted herself in front of Mr Gould on her long legs, throwing her dark plait back over her shoulder.

'*I'm* first. I'm the oldest.'

'So you are!' Mr Gould said, flustered at being found

in the wrong. 'By a whisker. Right, step up, Audrey.'

They lined up in front of the pile of builder's sand that they called their sandpit.

'Right, give your name and age.'

'Audrey – ten!'

'Surname?'

Audrey rolled her eyes. 'Whitehouse, of course.'

'Right, next. Look lively!' Sylvia's father sometimes said that Stanley Gould should have been in the Army, though up until now he never had been. He'd been too valuable in the factory during the Great War.

'Raymond Gould.' Raymond leapt into position, his pumps spraying gritty sand. 'Nine – nearly ten!'

'Sylvia Whitehouse – eight.' She was always much more biddable than Audrey and plodded into the line-up, happy just to be included with the others.

In the middle of this Marjorie Gould came outside. She stood with her arms folded over a vivid green dress, watching the military line-up of the children.

'Oh, Stan, leave 'em be,' she said in her easy voice. 'Let them come and have some lemonade – I've got it all ready – and a bit of cake.'

'We're in the middle of something, Marjorie,' Stanley said. 'They can have a reward when they've done some work.'

Marjorie went off, shaking her head. 'Work... They're only kids, Stanley!'

'Now, next!' Stanley Gould commanded.

Raymond's little brother looked very uncertain and they hustled him into line. Sylvia took pity on him, whispering, 'Say your name, and how old you are.'

'Laurie Gould . . .' He looked at Sylvia with anxious grey eyes and quietly inserted his little hand into hers. 'Seven!'

There were only the four of them then, although Mrs Gould must have been carrying Paul at the time, but they didn't know that. Jack's arrival was a good way off yet.

'Right,' Mr Gould said, hands on his waist. His fore-arms, below the rolled-up sleeves of his shirt, were covered in dark hair. 'Now, what do I get if I add Raymond and Audrey together?'

Sylvia tensed. Her hands started to feel clammy. This was when Mr Gould's games stopped being fun. She had not the faintest idea what the answer was. In fact, she didn't even realize he was talking about a number. She pictured a strange creature with four arms and four legs, with both Audrey's and Raymond's heads. The same cold dread filled her that she felt at school. She was about to be caught out and punished. She found she was gripping Laurie's hand as tightly as he was hers.

'You get nineteen,' Audrey said straight away. Her handsome face looked back at Mr Gould with something like defiance.

'And what if I take Laurie away from Sylvia?'

'One!' Audrey cried.

Sylvia was beginning to feel thoroughly fed up with Audrey, though at least it meant Mr Gould might not ask her his horrible questions. Although they weren't at school now, and no one would stripe her hand with a ruler until it smarted, like Miss Patchett did, she was already feeling churned up with nerves. Fortunately Audrey had also had enough of Mr Gould and his numbers.

'Can we have some lemonade now?' she asked.

Stanley looked disappointed at their lack of stamina. 'I think you mean: *please may we* . . . Go on then,' he said. 'Boys, we'll carry on with this later.'

No wonder Raymond and Laurie had both won places at the grammar school. When Paul was born, they were told he was a 'mongol'. It was some time before Sylvia had any idea what that meant. When they were at last allowed to see baby Paul – she and Audrey vying to be the first to look into the pram – she could see that his eyes were a bit different, that was all. It didn't seem to be so bad, she thought. But Stanley Gould knew what it meant and saw it as a curse – probably from God, because it was hard to know who else to blame. He seemed to believe that God might be as spiteful as that, and didn't know what to do with a child who wasn't clever. It had taken years for him even to begin to come to terms with it. For a long time he didn't even like Marjorie to take Paul out of the house, which of course upset her.

As she grew up, Sylvia often wondered why Dad and Stanley were friends. They were forever arguing. For a start, Stanley was a staunch member of the Church of England, while Ted said he wasn't having 'any of that old claptrap'. And that was before you got to their views on politics, the education of girls (which Stanley Gould thought was basically a waste of everybody's time) or the best way to grow carrots. But the two of them drank together, went for long bike rides, played the odd game of cribbage and chewed the fat contentiously over the garden wall while their wives rolled their eyes. Sylvia realized, eventually, that they thrived on their arguments. Maybe that's how she and Audrey had learned to fall out all the time.

Despite pressurizing his sons, Mr Gould had a kindly side to him and could be a tease. It was he who had nicknamed Sylvia 'Wizzy' because of her dark, flyaway curls. The name stuck and her own family started calling her 'Wizz' sometimes as well.

But that afternoon stayed painfully pressed into Sylvia's memory and one reason was that Raymond, who was usually quite kind, had been *un*kind. Audrey had managed to stop Mr Gould's number games, but Raymond wanted to carry on after the lemonade and cake.

'What are nine nines?' he demanded. He was good at tables, and so was Audrey.

'Eighty-one,' Audrey answered smartly. She and Sylvia were kneeling, tunnelling their hands into the pile of reddish sand. They gave each other a shove every so often, if one felt the other was too close. 'Get off, that's my bit!' 'No – you get off.'

Sylvia loved playing with the sand and resented Raymond carrying on like this. She kept her head down.

'What about six sevens, Sylvia?' he demanded.

Sylvia pretended she didn't hear him.

'Come on,' Raymond said, standing over her. 'It's easy!'

'Sylvia can't do numbers and things,' Audrey said in her superior voice. 'She can't even *read*.'

Sylvia hid further under her cloud of hair to hide the red heat seeping through her cheeks. She squeezed handfuls of the coarse sand, longing to hit Audrey over the head with something. They knew she was bad at letters and numbers! They were so *mean*. None of them knew what it was like to see a mass of letters merge into a swimming chaos in front of her eyes until she was in such a panic she couldn't think at all. With all her being she hated Raymond at that moment – and Audrey even more. But she felt too small and shamed to fight back.

'Six sevens are forty-two,' Audrey said airily. 'It's no good asking Wizz.'

'Sylvia's *stupid*,' Raymond said. He stood rocking from foot to foot, chorusing, 'Stupid-stupid Sylvia! Sylvia's a du-unce!'

Then Audrey joined in the chant, hopping from foot to foot in time with the words. 'Stupid-stupid Sylvia! Sylvia's a du-unce!'

She thought she even heard Laurie join in, until she was surrounded by their jeering voices. Of course they teased each other often, but not like this. Not with this mean, humiliating nastiness. The words echoed in her head, filling her as if she would never be able to get rid of them.

Sylvia got to her feet, keeping her head down so that she didn't have to look at their mocking, superior faces. All she wanted was to crawl somewhere dark so that she could curl up and never come out. Trying to keep from sobbing out loud, she hurried away, down to the gap where you could walk through between the wall and the railway fence and into their own garden.

'I'm *not* stupid,' she growled in a fierce little voice. 'I'm not, I'm *not*! I hate you . . . *I hate you*.' She ran into the house, hardly able to see where she was going through her tears.

Her teachers never understood that she was willing, but not able. Words and numbers ganged up on her. When they learned about the parts of flowers and fruit, everything went well until Miss Patchett wrote names by the arrows, pointing into the parts, and then Sylvia was lost. She sat staring at her slate in despair. A moment later she realized, to her terror, that Miss Patchett was standing over her.

'What's that?' Miss Patchett pointed her scrawny finger. She was quite a young teacher, with wire spectacles, hollow cheeks and stony eyes.

'It's . . .' The named bits of the flower scrambled in Sylvia's head. There'd been something beginning with S, she was sure. 'It's a staple, Miss.'

Miss Patchett slapped the left side of Sylvia's head so hard that for a moment she couldn't see straight.

'It's a *stamen*. As I have written perfectly clearly on the blackboard.' She pointed witheringly. 'See? *Stamen*.' This brought another slap with it.

The other children sniggered.

'Yes, Miss,' Sylvia murmured. She couldn't see anything now through her tears.

'Thank heavens your sister's not like you!' Miss Patchett said. 'A *staple*,' she went on, witheringly, 'is for attaching one sheet of paper to another. Go on, girl – write the proper label on your flower.'

Almost beside herself with panic, Sylvia leaned

towards the slate, her hand so sweaty she could hardly hold the pencil. She breathed in. S. It began with S. She managed to write a wavery S, but then couldn't think for the life of her what came next. There was a twinge in her lower body and she was frightened she might wet herself. Miss Patchett was leaning over her. Sylvia could smell her greasy hair and body odour, blended with the stale tea on her breath. She squeezed her eyes closed, fidgeting to avert the urgent pressure from her bladder, and said 'stamen' to herself over and over again.

'Come *on*, girl,' Miss Patchett insisted, standing tall again. 'Keep still! What comes next?' The class had gone quiet. Sylvia felt as if she was the only person in the world apart from her bony teacher with her nasty, slapping hands.

'I don't know,' Sylvia was about to say when Jane, next to her, dared to breathe, 'T.'

'T,' Sylvia said grasping this like a life raft.

'T! Well, write it down then, girl.'

'A,' Jane sighed next. How Miss Patchett didn't hear her, Sylvia would never know. She was able to sit still now, for the crisis had passed.

With Jane's help she managed to get to the end of the word without another slap. Miss Patchett moved away and Sylvia gave her friend the smile of the rescued.

She could *draw* a flower perfectly. Why could she not do the rest? She didn't know, and no one seemed to understand. She hated school, every part of it except playtime, when she and Jane and some of the other girls played jackstones and skipping in the yard, at the other end from the rowdy boys. When she came home it was like being let out of prison. She tried to shut school right out of her mind so that the thought of it did not pollute the rest of her life.

But the teasing at home was different. The humiliation and unfairness of it bit deeply into her. She felt it as actual pain in her body, an ache that spread all over her. As she ran inside, Mom heard her sobs and came out to see what was going on.

'Oi, where're you off to, Miss?' Pauline asked as her daughter tore up the stairs. She stood in her apron, looking up. 'Have you hurt yourself?'

Sylvia curled up tightly on her bed in the room she then shared with Audrey. Hearing her mother's steps on the staircase, she tensed, afraid this might mean more mockery or punishment.

'Wizzy?'

Sylvia opened one eye. Mom was standing at the door. She looked comforting, with her round pink cheeks and her auburn hair in thick plaits, pinned around her head and crossing over at the front. Sylvia desperately wanted someone to understand. Her reports from school were very poor, and her parents sighed over them in a way that Sylvia took to mean: *Why can't you be like the Goulds? Or at least like Audrey?*

Mom came and sat on the bed. Her pinner was dusted with flour and there was a whiff of onions about her as well.

'What's going on?' she said. 'I thought you were all playing next door?'

Sylvia squeezed her eyes closed and pulled herself into an even tighter coil. Words burst out of her. 'Raymond called me stupid. And Audrey! I *hate* them. Both of them are pigs.'

Her mother gave a long sigh and Sylvia felt her hand rest on her skinny shoulder.

'You don't want to take any notice,' Pauline said. 'Your sister should know better than to talk like that – and Raymond. I don't know why you and Audrey can't get on a bit better.'

Sylvia pushed herself up, limbs stiff with outrage. 'I *can't* not take any notice! They're calling me horrible names and . . . And I'm *not* stupid!'

Mom was looking at her with a tender expression. She raised her hand, and Sylvia felt her mother's work-roughened, oniony thumb rubbing away the tears from her hot cheeks.

'Look at your little face,' her mother said fondly. She

dropped her hand again and sighed. 'I know you're not stupid, bab,' she said. 'That's the worst of it. Your father and I've talked about it. You're as bright as a button. So why can't you read and write properly, like the others?'

Sylvia hung her head. 'I don't know. I just can't.'

Pauline had words with Marjorie Gould. Could she please ask Raymond not to be nasty and upset Sylvia? After that, they all kept off the subject. They never got to the bottom of Sylvia's problems. Year by year she struggled on.

The one person she felt at ease with was little Laurie Gould. He was younger than her and left-handed, so he struggled with writing. Stanley did not like having a left-handed son. In his day you would have been made to sit on your left hand and write with your right one – that was his attitude. Under the pretence of Sylvia helping Laurie learn to read, she would help him with his little story books; and he helped her, with Sylvia learning along with him. She did get the hang of reading and writing eventually, but she was slow at it. After Paul was born, even Stanley Gould stopped keeping on about success and 'getting on', now that he had a son who had little prospect of it.

Sylvia dreamed of the wonderful day when she would

be able to walk out of school and never come back. At last, when she was fourteen, the day arrived and it was one of the happiest of her life. She took her reference and headed away from the place of shame and humiliation, to a job – any job that did not involve reading or writing. At first she worked in factories and then a laundry. No one made her read or write. The work was boring, but restful. No one went out of their way to make her feel stupid.

Raymond floundered at the grammar school and did not pass his exams with much distinction. He couldn't sit exams without being paralysed by nerves, which Sylvia's dad said was obviously Stanley's fault ('the silly bugger'). Raymond left school when he was sixteen, almost as glad as Sylvia to get away from it.

Only when she was much older did Sylvia realize that Raymond's nastiness that day was in some measure Raymond passing onto her what he felt about himself.

Pam Weaver

Pam Weaver has written numerous articles and short stories for magazines including *Take a Break, Take a Break Fiction Feast, Woman's Weekly Fiction Special, Best, My Weekly* and *The People's Friend*. Her book *Bath Times & Nursery Rhymes* tells of her experiences as a nursery nurse and Hyde Park nanny and was a *Sunday Times* bestseller.

Pam's saga novels, *There's Always Tomorrow, Better Days Will Come, Pack Up Your Troubles* and *For Better For Worse*, are set in Worthing during the austerity years.

Pam's inspiration comes from her love of people and their stories and her passion for the town of Worthing. With the sea on one side and the Downs on the other, Worthing has a scattering of small villages within its urban sprawl, and in some cases tight-knit communities, making it an ideal setting for the modern saga.

More Books by Pam Weaver

Bath Times & Nursery Rhymes
There's Always Tomorrow
Better Days Will Come
Pack Up Your Troubles
For Better For Worse

Mary Wood

Born the thirteenth child of fifteen to a middle-class mother and an East End barrow boy, Mary Wood's childhood was a mixture of love and poverty. This encouraged her to develop a natural empathy with the less fortunate and a fascination with social history. Throughout her life Mary has held various posts in catering and office roles, and in the Probation service, while bringing up her four children. Mary now has numerous grandchildren, step-grandchildren and great-grandchildren. An avid reader, she first put pen to paper in 1989 whilst nursing her mother through her last months, but didn't become successful until she began to self-publish her novels in the late 2000s.

More Books by Mary Wood

The Breckton trilogy:

An Unbreakable Bond
To Catch a Dream
Tomorrow Brings Sorrow

Time Passes Time

The Cotton Mill saga:

Judge Me Not

TIME PASSES TIME
by Mary Wood

Theresa's War. It is 1941, and the world is at war. Young Theresa Crompton is left devastated after giving up her illegitimate child and joins the Special Operations Executive, an organization of undercover agents working behind enemy lines. Her mission is to assist a Resistance group run by the handsome Pierre Rueben and it is not long before they fall in love. Soon Theresa becomes pregnant but circumstances tear Pierre and the child from Theresa.

London, 1963. An older Theresa is haunted by her experiences during the war. In her damaged mind, the past tangles with the present and Theresa soon feels she has to make a terrifying decision. Her long-lost children are seeking answers. Will Theresa be reunited with them, before it's too late?

A thrilling and emotive saga by top-ten Kindle bestselling ebook author of the Breckton trilogy, Mary Wood. *Time Passes Time* is perfect for fans of Margaret Dickinson, Nadine Dorries and Lily Baxter.

Read on for an extract from
Time Passes Time by Mary Wood

One

War is a Tangled Memory
Linked to the Present

'Hey, let go, you old bag . . .'

Theresa staggered. The hooded young men in front of her grabbed at her bag. Fear paralysed her. Unreleased screams filled her head . . . *My secrets . . . Oh, God!*

Images flashed into her memory, but faded away into a haze of confusion as she tried to decipher the snippets of information that her brain managed to filter. She struggled to make sense of them and to separate *the now* from *the past*. Her fragile mind had little capacity to give her reality, having never recovered from the mental breakdown she'd suffered after the suicide of Terence, her twin brother, in 1958. And now it took her back in time, compounding her fear as she desperately sought for answers: *What's happening? Are they SS?*

Frail, and old beyond her years, every bone in her body hurt. The sockets of her arms burned as she fought valiantly. *Stay quiet,* she told herself. *Name and number only . . . Don't give in.*

A sudden thought trembled a deeper dread through her. The training officer of the Special Operations Executive had warned, 'If caught, you may be subjected to torture.' He'd listed several possibilities, but one had stuck in her mind: 'Sometimes they resort to pulling out your fingernails . . .'

Her terror of this often catapulted her from sleep in the middle of the night. How close she'd come to such a fate! Betrayed and captured, she'd felt the chafing of the irons that had held her and had sweated the cold sweat of terror as she'd thought her fate the same as her fellow SOE officers, Eliane, Yolande, Madeleine and Noor. Just saying their names was an honour, as they were the bravest women she'd ever known. The Germans had captured and executed them. After forcing the women to kneel in pairs, they had shot them in the head.

With these thoughts intensifying her fear, the cloying darkness of the cell the Germans had thrown her into enclosed her once more, as did the desperate feeling of being alone. Alone and about to die.

Was it happening again? Were these Nazis? Had they found her? Would she tell them what she knew? *Please, God, help me not to . . .*

'For Christ's sake! She's got some strength for an old 'un.'

'What's that she said? Did she call us *Nazis*? The bleedin' old cow . . .'

Theresa's head flew back with the force of the blow. Her fingers felt the cold pavement slab but could not prevent her fall. A boot hovered over her hand.

'Give us yer bag, you stupid old witch. Let go . . .'

The boot came down. Bones cracked. '14609, Theresa Laura Crompton, Officer . . .'

'Christ, she's bleedin' mad. She's saying something about being an officer. Ha, she must be ninety-odd. Bleedin' officer, my hat. This is 1963, you stupid old bat! Get her bag, quick, she's let go of it. Come on, leg it.'

Pain seared her. Jumbled questions frustrated her: *Is this London? Is the war over? Oh, dear God, what year did he say it was?*

No answers came, only the knowledge that she had lost the fight and that her attackers had gone. So too had the spirit that had powered her efforts. In its place lay a pit of despair.

The leg she lay on started to throb. She had to shift position to release the pressure on her hip. As she did, an agony beyond endurance brought vomit to her throat. She swallowed it down. Felt the choking sting it left in its wake. How could Derwent have thought her capable of doing this job? Yes, she spoke French, and yes, she knew the country well. But she wasn't brave enough . . . She wasn't brave enough . . .

And what about the mission? *Pierre will be waiting . . . Oh, Pierre, my love. Please, God, keep him safe from capture. And our son, protect our son.* For hadn't she put them in grave danger? Those Nazis had her bag, her papers and the secrets she was charged with keeping. 'Never write anything down!' they'd told her. She'd disobeyed that golden rule. She'd written everything down. She'd told where her baby son and his grandparents were and that they were Jews. The Germans would . . . Oh, God! Why had she done it? Why had she compiled a complete record of her life from the day she'd had to give her first child away? Now the Nazis would know everything: the rendezvous point, the codes . . . *Millions will die . . .* But, no, that wasn't right. *It was 1953 when I began to write about it all – long after the war. Oh, why do my thoughts swim away from me?*

A voice with a twang of Cockney to it broke into her thoughts, 'Blimey, it's that Miss Crompton. Have you fallen, love? It's alright, don't be afraid . . .'

It sounds like Rita, but no, Rita wouldn't call me 'Miss Crompton'. Rita loved her and called her nice names. Rita was a Land Girl on her brother's farm. They were having an affair, a liaison. Exciting, different . . . *Oh, God! Stop it, stop this confusion . . . That was then. Rita is old now and smells of drink. She can be cruel and demands money. Has Rita sent these people to hurt me?*

'Her nose is bleeding, Mum. She's shaking . . .'

'Okay, Trace, don't just stand there. Nip across to that

phone box and dial 999. Now then, love, help will be here soon. You keep yourself still. Bleedin' 'ell, this is a turn-up, but you're safe now.'

Theresa's trepidation intensified as her yesterdays crowded her brain once more: *These people seem to know me. Are they the ones who will be nice to me and try to gain my confidence?*

'Don't be scared. We ain't going to hurt yer, love.'

Opening her eyes she tried to focus, but the glare of the sun overwhelmed her and she snapped them shut again. Before doing so she'd seen a blue light flashing. She'd never known the Germans to use such a warning sign. Would they take her back to Dachau? Would they shoot her? Or – *no, dear God, not that . . . Not burned alive in the oven as they'd done to one poor girl. Oh God, help me!* More voices. How many were there? Men's voices, trying to soothe her and to calm her. *I must stay strong. Sing, that's the thing. Concentrate on a song.* 'There'll be blue birds over . . . Tomorrow, just you wait and see . . .'

'That's the spirit, love. My old mum used to tell us to sing when we were afraid or in pain. I'm Marcus, and I'm just going to give you an injection to make you more comfortable, then we need to put a splint on that leg. We think you may have fractured it. Lie still now.'

'No . . . No . . .' She tried to push the man's hand away, but couldn't. Her thigh stung; her head swam. *Oh, God, no!* They had warned her about this new method. 'They may inject you,' they'd said. 'It's not lethal, but it relaxes you and you are no longer on your guard. If they do, try to think of something important and concentrate on it. Shut everything else out.'

'Don't like needles, eh? Nearly done. You'll be better for it, love.'

Pierre, oh, Pierre, I have let you down. Please, God, don't let them capture him. He will face certain death! No, I couldn't bear it . . . I love you, Pierre. The words he had said to her came into her mind: *'Tu es le souffle de mon corps. Le sang qui coule dans mes veines et la vie dans mon coeur.' That is what I will think of.* She could hear his voice, and drank his words deep into her as she said them in her mind over and over: 'You are the breath in my body. The blood that courses through my veins and the life inside my heart.'

Two

A Journey into the Past

''Ere, sis, you said you wanted a new bleedin' handbag, so I bleedin' got yer one.'

The brown, square-shaped bag landed in Lizzie's lap. She could see it wasn't new, and this set up a worry in her. Turning it over she noticed, though old-fashioned, it showed hardly any sign of wear. The leather, soft and of good quality, was gathered into a brass trim with a tortoiseshell clasp that she had to twist to undo. As she did, a fusty smell clogged her nose. Sifting through the contents – some papers, a few exercise books rolled up and secured with an elastic band, and several photos, all yellowing with age – she found the bag didn't contain a purse or anything of value. But then, she hadn't expected it to. Ken or his cronies would have removed anything of that nature.

'Look at you, ferreting already. I knew it would suit yer. You're a right old square.'

'I ain't—'

'Well, what's with the Perry Como, then?' A screech set her teeth on edge as Ken shoved the arm of the gramophone, causing the needle to slide across the long-playing record. Perry's 'Can't Help Falling in Love' stretched and distorted on the last line.

'Don't do that! You know it scratches the record! And I ain't a square. Rita put that on before she fell asleep. I just didn't bother to change it, that's all.'

'Huh, in that case yer won't like rummaging through that crappy old stuff, then. No one who's *with it* likes the stuff you like. Who digs history and antiques these days? Accept it, me little skin and blister: you're a square.'

Ken came towards her. A cold feeling of apprehension clenched her stomach muscles. She turned in her wheelchair, but what she saw gave her no hope of help from Rita. Slumped on the settee, dead to the world, Rita's lips flapped on every exhaled breath, filling the room with alcohol fumes. One slack arm rested on the empty gin bottle lying on the floor.

'What's up, darling? You look like a bleedin' caged animal. Don't yer like the present I got for yer?'

His voice soothed some of Lizzie's fear. It didn't hold a hint of what had fuelled her dread. His mood changes had her treading on eggshells. She didn't like how he talked at times, joking in a way she knew wasn't a joke about how, even though she was disabled, she shouldn't be deprived. At these times his body leaned closer than she was comfortable with, and his eyes sent messages she didn't want to read as he made out that one of his mates – the one he nicknamed Loopy Laurence – fancied her.

She kept her voice steady as she answered him. 'Course I do, but it's where you got it from that worries me.'

'Found it.'

She doubted that – more like *half-inched* it, as he called pinching stuff. He always used Cockney rhyming slang. It was as if he thought it added to the tough, bully-boy image he liked to portray. Snatching bags was a bit below his league, though, so he wouldn't have done the deed himself; he'd have got it from someone who owed him. It must have seemed strange to them, him wanting the bag as well as the valuables it contained.

Rita stirred and opened one eye. 'You bleedin' got it, then? How much were in it? The old cow's been a bit tight lately with what she'll give me.'

'Shut your mouth or I'll shut it for yer, you bleedin' drunk.'

'Don't talk to Rita like that, Ken . . .'

'Don't you bleedin' start or—' The shrill tone of

the phone cut his threat short. 'No! That'll be bloody Rednut. He can't do anything on his own.'

Relief slowed Lizzie's breath and released the tension in her as she heard him say he would meet Rednut in ten minutes. From what she picked up of the conversation, something had gone wrong with a collection. She didn't know the extent of Ken's dealings, but he'd talked about some of the known gangs running protection rackets and that kind of thing, but to what extent he was involved and exactly who with she wasn't sure. She knew he wasn't big-time, not in the league of the Krays and gangs like that, but she hated to think of what he did get up to. If she could get real proof, she would go to the police. But then, would she? Always conflict raged inside her where her brother was concerned, one minute wanting him to get caught, and the next praying for his safety.

'Right, I have to go. Will you be alright, love?' His tone surprised her. She'd thought she would bear the brunt of his anger at Rita and Rednut. Still might, but that didn't stop her retorting, 'If you would stop doing whatever it is you are up to, I would be.'

'Not that again. Whinge, whinge, whinge. You don't mind when I get things for you out of the proceeds, do you? Look at that chair. The National Health Service would never have got you one like it. You're such a bleedin' ungrateful sod!'

Taking hold of the handlebars and squeezing the lever set her wheelchair into motion. She needed to get out of his presence. He jumped in front of her. 'Where're you going?'

'To my room.'

'Look, sis, I brought the bag back for you, didn't I?'

His pleading look sickened her, but the softening of his attitude towards her gave her courage to take him to task again. 'Ken, it ain't right what you do, why can't yer see that? I know yer mean well, and think getting me things will make up for everything, but the way yer get them ain't right. I'd rather go without. What happened to the lady this belonged to? Is she hurt?'

'Lady? She ain't no bleedin' lady! I could tell yer tales. Anyway, Ken, where's me cut, then?'

This from Rita shocked her. *Rita knew the owner!* And by the sounds of things she'd helped to set up whatever Ken had done to get the bag.

'You'll get it when I'm good and bleedin' ready.' Ken had moved towards Lizzie's bedroom, a ground-floor room originally intended as a front room. A beam of sunlight shone through the door as he opened it for her. It lit a trail back to the sofa and glinted off the gin bottle. Ken stood still. His face held a look of contempt. 'That bag was a payment. I earned it for you, sis. I hurt no one. What others did, including her,' he pointed at Rita, 'ain't my fault. Christ, you're a bleedin' hypocrite, sis. Look how you're clinging to it, afraid I'll take it back, and yet you're on your high horse about *my* morals!'

As she passed him, tension and fear tightened her throat. *Please don't let him follow me in.*

He didn't. The door slammed shut behind her, giving her a feeling of safety from the threat of him, but the knowledge of why he did what he did completed the circle of her inner conflict. He wanted – no, *needed* – to get things for her to assuage the constant guilt that nagged at him over her disability, and it was this need that had started him down the road of his illegal activities.

Throwing the bag onto her bed, she let her head drop and screwed up her eyes. The latch to the part of her she kept locked away had shifted, letting in unwanted thoughts. She tried to fight them, but her mind ran back down the years. Shudders rippled through her as she saw again the blood – always the blood. Her mum's blood, spurting from her nose, her lip and her forehead. And Ken's, seeping through his shirt as their dad's belt lashed his back. The screams and the vile threats assaulted her ears afresh. Her dad's face, ugly with his intent, flashed into her mind, and she saw again his big, muscle-bound body dripping with sweat as he turned and aimed another blow at their mum as she tried to stop the onslaught on Ken. And into the memory came the moment when something had snapped inside her and had taken away her fear . . .

Her teeth clenched, as if they remembered independently of her how they had sunk into her dad's leg. The taste of the oil and gunk spilt onto his jeans came back to her. Its tang stretched her mouth and brought her Aunt Alice to her mind. Her dad had been mending Aunt Alice's car. Hate welled up in Lizzie. Alice should be the one to shoulder the guilt. She shouldn't have told their dad about Ken pinching from her purse. She'd have known what would happen. Mum would have sorted it on the quiet.

Lizzie held her ears, trying to block out the memory of her dad's howl of pain. Like the soundtrack to a horror movie, it had stayed with her down the years, filling her head each time she relived the scene. With it came the feeling of her hair being wrenched till she'd been forced to release her bite, and the sensation of hurtling through the air and down the stairwell. *He'd thrown her!* Her own dad had thrown her as if she was nothing. The world encompassing her had changed from the moment she'd hit the bottom step.

She'd never seen her mum again. A brain haemorrhage that night had taken her. Her dad, wanted for her murder, had been missing ever since.

Rita, her mum's youngest sister, had taken her and Ken on, which couldn't have been an easy thing to do. Rita had come back from Australia after her man had conned her out of everything she had. Knowing what had happened to them hadn't stopped her going, but she'd thought one of the other family members would take care of them. Finding her, a fifteen-year-old, in a children's home and sixteen-year-old Ken in Borstal had enraged her. She'd not given up until she had them both with her, falling out with all of her sisters and brothers in the process and never speaking to them again. Five of them, there were – well, five still alive though there had been ten altogether. There'd also been two aunts on her dad's side, and not one of them had stepped in to help her and her brother. They would have let them rot.

She and Ken hadn't known Rita very well, and their mum hadn't spoken much of her. Their dad had referred to her, for as long as she could remember, as 'that bag in jail', and as being no better than her mum's brother Alf, but that hadn't meant much at the time. Now it didn't seem possible that Rita coming into their lives was just four short years ago. It had been wonderful at the time, but things deteriorated when Rita took to the drink and Ken's carry-ons caused friction. Ken had no respect for Rita.

These last thoughts held in them the misery of their lives today, but they still couldn't hold a candle to what had gone before, nor stop the quiver of her nerves when she wondered about the future. But dwelling on it didn't help. Physically shaking herself free of the terrible recollections, she felt the pain of her nails digging into her palms. Taking her time, she unfurled each cramped finger from the tight fist they had curled into, took some deep breaths, and wiped the sweat and tears from her face.

The bag came into focus. Leaning forward, she pulled it towards her. Maybe she could get a clue as to the owner by going through it. An address, perhaps, though if she did find that she'd have to post the bag back to whomever it belonged to, as taking it might implicate Ken.

A frayed, faded-green, wartime ID card lay on top of the pile of paperwork that had dropped from the up-turned bag. Opening it revealed a black-and-white image of a young woman. Her face, though not smiling, was beautiful. Her hair – old-fashioned in its style: rolled on the top and falling into soft waves – caught the light in its dark colour. Something about the eyes and the expression told of this girl having hidden depths and a strong determination. She read the information: *Theresa Laura Crompton, born: 23.3.1911, York, United Kingdom.*

Looking at the date stamped on the card told her Theresa would have been thirty at the time. That would make her fifty-two now. *Oh, God, please don't let her have been hurt . . .*

Something had fallen out from inside the ID card: a similar document in French, though smaller and brown in colour and with the same picture inside. And yet, it bore a different name: *Olivia Danchanté, date de naissance: 24.5.1911, Paris, France.* Puzzled and with her interest piqued, Lizzie shuffled through the rest. An envelope tied with ribbon revealed several scribbled notes, again written in French. If only she'd paid more attention to languages in school. But, excelling in history, English and maths, she had given little to anything that bored her, and her education had been cut short after . . . No, she'd not let those thoughts in again. They had already taken her spirit and shredded it.

Laying the letters down, she picked up the photos. Some of them were in sepia, while others were in black and white. There was one of Theresa or Olivia – confusing with the identity cards showing different names – with a young man of the same height and very similar in looks and age, around twenty to twenty-six-ish at the time. She'd have thought them to be brother and sister, as there was another photo of them with an older couple that had *Terence and me with Mater and Pater* written on the back, but in this picture, their way of leaning close and how he looked at her suggested a lover; turning it over, Lizzie read, *1938, Terence and me at Hensal Grange.*

There were others of Theresa/Olivia with young people in uniform, and in a separate envelope there was one of her in a man's arms. They were holding a baby, one of a few months old, and looking into each other's eyes – clearly lovers. Husband and wife, even? In this one she noted that Theresa/Olivia had pencilled a Margaret Lockwood beauty spot on her cheek, and that she had exaggerated the fullness of her lips with her lipstick. This made Lizzie smile. As a young woman, she must have been a romantic and a follower of the latest fashions. A happier thought from Lizzie's past surfaced, bringing the image of her mum all dressed up and ready to go out with her dad and looking similar to the young woman in the photo. Her dad, looking dapper in his dark suit and white shirt and with his white silk scarf dangling from his neck, had leaned forward and tickled her with the scarf's tassels. The memory cheered her as she looked at a photo taken in a field. Remnants of a picnic could be seen in the background. Theresa/Olivia was bending forward with her arms outstretched. Her skirt clung to her legs at the front and billowed out at the back. It must have been a windy day. A little boy held on to a wooden truck as if he might let go and walk towards her, but he looked only around ten or eleven months old. His face was a picture of joy. On the back it said, *my son, Jacques, August 1944*. And yet another of the man on his own – a foreign-looking man, with floppy hair parted on one side, nice eyes and a handsome face, though his smile, tilted to one side, gave him a rakish look. This connected with Lizzie. She loved a sense of humour in a man. On the back of this photo she read, *Pierre Rueben, October, 1943, the father of my son.* Then in French, and in a different handwriting, *Je t'aime, jamais m'oublier.* With the little she remembered from her French lessons, she could just make out that this said something along the lines of: *I love you, never forget me.*

Putting these to one side, Lizzie picked up the roll of exercise books. The strong elastic band rasped along the cover of the outer book as she forced it to release a bulk that was almost too much for it.

With edges resisting her attempts to straighten them, the books – ten in all – lay curled in front of her. On the top one, written in neat handwriting, she read:

MY WAR – MY LOVE – MY LIFE
Theresa Crompton

With her imagination fired, Lizzie opened the book. On the first page she read how Theresa had begun the memoir in September 1953, to commemorate the tenth birthday of her lost son Jacques, whose whereabouts she did not know. The milestone of his birthday had prompted her to write about her life and her war, as now the world was at peace she felt she could hurt no one by doing so.

Even though she did not know Theresa, it saddened

Lizzie to read that as she wrote Theresa was fragile in her mind and body and hoped the writing of everything down would act as a cathartic exercise for her.

The dedication fascinated her and she felt her heart clench with sadness.

This work is dedicated to Pierre Rueben, my love and my life. And to our son, Jacques Rueben, and to my first child, my Olivia, who will probably never know who I am but whom I have never stopped loving. Not a day passes that I do not think of her and of Pierre and Jacques, and of course Terence, my beloved late twin brother.

To Lizzie, these words held a story in themselves. One of a lonely woman, left without everyone she'd ever loved. But why? So many questions she hoped the books would answer.

KING'S COLLEGE HOSPITAL – LONDON 1963

'So, no one has come forward to claim the old girl, then, nurse?'

'No, Officer, and we think her general frailty is giving us the wrong impression of her age. She tells us she is fifty-two, but as you can see, she looks nearer seventy. Who she is, is a mystery. One moment she is Theresa Crompton, and the next she says she is Olivia Danchanté. But then, she is obviously suffering some kind of mental illness or dementia. She seems to be reliving the war years, talking of the Nazis and someone called Pierre. Sometimes she speaks in English, sometimes in French. Poor thing thinks we are the Germans and have captured her. She's terrified.'

'That would explain her house. The whole place is barricaded with old newspapers and cardboard boxes stacked from floor to ceiling. There's just a small gap to get in and out through, and the smell ... Well, anyway, as of yet we haven't found her bag or any private papers, but the woman who found her confirmed she is Miss Crompton.'

Theresa lay still, her fear compounded. *What are they saying? They've been in the house? How did they find it? What of Monsieur et Madame de Langlois? Smell ...? Have they gassed them? Please, God, no ... But they haven't found my papers. Oh, Pierre, they don't know of you yet. My darling, please wait. I will get to you. How brave you are, my darling.*

'Oh dear, she's getting agitated again. It's alright, love. Miss Crompton, come on. You're safe now. You're in hospital. No one can hurt you. Look, I'm sorry, Officer, you can see how distressed she is. I'll have to fetch the doctor. She needs a sedative. There's nothing more I can tell you at the moment anyway, but if she does have a lucid moment and gives us some indication of what happened to her, I'll contact you.'

'I'd like to try to talk to her if I can ...'

'Sorry, not until the doctor says so. I won't be a moment.'

Fear once more gripped Theresa as she listened to this conversation. *Oh, God, they want to talk to me. Pierre, take over my thoughts. Help me through this.*

The scent of the meadow on that Sunday afternoon when they'd picnicked filled her nostrils. Was it last week? Her mind gave her the moment she'd said, 'Look, Jacques is sleeping. We have tired him out.' Laughing, Pierre had picked a buttercup and she saw in her mind's eye how the sun had reflected the gold of the flower as she'd held it under his chin. His giggle at her funny British custom tinkled in her ears. '*Ma chérie*, how can a reflection tell if I like butter or no?'

Explaining how the myth amused children in England on sunny picnic outings had brought a happiness into her as she'd thought of her and Terence, but, as always, thinking of him had prickled her conscience. For hadn't they tainted such innocent moments?

Pierre left her no time to let her thoughts drift to those painful parts of her inner self as he'd gently laid her back onto the soft grass and lifted her face to his. 'Let me show you a good French tradition, *ma chérie*.' His kisses had reeled her senses. Her body had yielded to his with a passion that released her very soul from the shackles that held it. But something gave her the truth of the moment and brought her back to now, and she knew it hadn't stayed free for long.

Diane Allen's Sherry Trifle

Serves 6

160 g (6 oz) jam Swiss roll, cut into thick slices,
or 160 g (6 oz) packet of trifle sponges

5 tablespoons sweet sherry

1 x 135 g (5 oz) block of raspberry jelly, made up to
¾ pint (425 ml) following the packet instructions

280 g (10 oz) of fresh raspberries and
a few extra for decoration

500 ml (18 fl. oz) of home-made custard (*see below*)
or 1 packet of ready-made custard

500 ml (18 fl. oz) of whipping cream, softly whipped

Handful of flaked almonds

*The trifle can be made in one large dish
or in individual glasses.*

Line the bottom of the dish or glasses with the cake
slices or trifle sponges. Sprinkle with the sherry and
leave to soak for 5 minutes.

Lay the raspberries over the cake and press lightly to release the juices. Pour the liquid jelly over the sponge and fruit and place in a refrigerator until the jelly is set.

Once set, spoon over the semi-cold custard, making a thick layer.

Finally, finish with a thick layer of whipped cream, either spooned or piped using a piping bag. Decorate with raspberries and flaked almonds.

Custard Sauce Recipe

140 ml (5 fl. oz) milk
240 ml (8.5 fl. oz) double cream
50 g (2 oz) caster sugar
6 large egg yolks
1 vanilla pod, split and seeds removed

Place the milk and cream and one teaspoon of the sugar into a pan. Bring to a gentle simmer: once simmering, turn the heat to its lowest.

In a large heatproof bowl, place the remaining sugar and the egg yolks and whisk until light, creamy and pale in colour.

Slowly whisking by hand, pour the warmed milk into the egg mixture.

Add the seeds from the vanilla pod and then return the custard to the saucepan and stir constantly over a low heat until it thickens. Do not rush this process, or the custard will curdle or, even worse, burn.

Finally, once thickened, remove from heat and pass through a sieve, then leave until needed.

Rita Bradshaw's Christmas Cake Recipe

Christmas cake is universal, I know, but this particular Durham recipe is a north-east special and once sampled is impossible to resist.

170 g (6 oz) butter
170 g (6 oz) lard
170 g (6 oz) soft brown sugar
170 g (6 oz) caster sugar
6 eggs
1 tbsp mixed spice
1 tsp ground cinnamon
340 g (12 oz) plain flour
225 g (8 oz) each of sultanas, currants and raisins
85 g (3 oz) each of glacé cherries, mixed peel, chopped walnuts and ground almonds
1 tbsp black treacle
1 bottle of Guinness

Also prepare: 23-cm / 9-inch cake tin lined with three layers of greaseproof paper.

Cream together the butter, lard, brown sugar and caster sugar for at least 10 minutes – preferably 15,

if you can manage it. Add the eggs, beating well between each addition.

Sieve the flour with the spices and fold into the butter mixture.

Add the fruit, peel and walnuts and mix well before adding the ground almonds. Fold these in and distribute evenly. Stir in the treacle, and enough Guinness to make a soft dropping consistency. Have a good sniff – Christmas in a bowl!

Put the mixture into the cake tin and drop the tin sharply onto a hard surface to knock out any air pockets. Don't forget to do this.

Tie six thicknesses of brown paper round the outside of the cake tin, leaving the top uncovered. Place the tin on the bottom shelf of the oven and bake for 1½ hours at gas mark 3, 160°C, then for a further 2-2½ hours on gas mark 2, 140°C.

Begin testing the cake mixture after 3½ hours; a skewer inserted carefully into the middle of the cake should come out clean.

Once removed from the oven, leave the cake to cool and turn out of the tin only when cold. Add marzipan and icing sugar if desired, but delicious perfectly naked (the cake, not you!).

Margaret Dickinson's Plum Pudding Recipe

This plum pudding recipe was originally made by my grandmother and has been passed down the family. I still use this recipe every year – and it has become a firm favourite!

2 lb finely grated carrot
2 lb fine breadcrumbs
2 lb finely chopped suet
2 lb moist sugar
2 lb sultanas
2 lb Valencia raisins
2 lb currants
¼ lb lemon and citrus peel (mixed)
2 oz sweet almonds
3 tbsp marmalade
5 eggs, beaten

Mix carrot, breadcrumbs, suet and sugar together and leave to moisten for 24 hours

Wash and dry and seed raisins, then wash and stalk the other fruit before mixing all the ingredients together – with the beaten eggs to be added last.

Grease 5 or 6 pudding bowls and fill three-quarters of the way up.

Steam for 2 hours.

Annie Murray's Celery, Apricot and Walnut Stuffing

My mum always had the ambition to be a cook, but having left school at fourteen during the Depression of the 1930s and being one of six children, it was straight into a Coventry factory as a filing clerk for her. In the 1970s, she spotted the fact that the French cookery school Cordon Bleu were offering a course, week by week, in magazines you could buy at the newsagent's. This was her kind of creativity and off she went! Our diet swiftly became more interesting. This turkey stuffing is a recipe she has used ever since and which I now use myself – it is one of the tastes of Christmas for me. It's easy to make and very handy if you have a vegetarian in the family, as it also makes a very tasty veggie bake.

50 g (2 oz) dried apricots (soaked overnight)
40 g (1½ oz) butter
2 onions, chopped finely
1 small head of celery (thinly sliced)

115 g (4 oz) walnuts, chopped
1½ teacups breadcrumbs
1 tbsp parsley, chopped

Drain apricots and cut each half into 3–4 pieces.

Melt butter in a pan, add the onions, then cover and cook until soft. Add the celery, apricots and walnuts. Cook for about 4 minutes over a brisk heat, stirring continuously, then turn into a bowl. When cool, add the breadcrumbs and parsley. Season to taste.

When ready, insert into turkey!

Mince Pies – Recommended by Pam Weaver

I am what my mother used to call a 'plain cook'. I'm not interested in pretty-looking food but I love good taste. For some years I have made my own mince-meat for mince pies, and although it may not look the way we expect in the jar, the taste is amazing.

225 g (8 oz) cooking apples
225 g (8 oz) currants
225 g (8 oz) sultanas
110 g (4 oz) glacé cherries
110 g (4 oz) candied peel
110 g (4 oz) chopped walnuts
225 g (8 oz) unsalted butter
450 g (1 lb) demerara sugar
2 tsp mixed spice
150 ml (4 fl. oz) brandy (I usually measure
this ingredient with a shaky hand!)

Peel and core the apples and cut into small chunks. Add to all the other ingredients (holding back the brandy) in a large bowl and mix together. Stir in the brandy and mix well. Put into clean jars[*] and cover as for jam.

Leave for 2–3 weeks before using and stir well when you open. A liquid forms at the bottom of the jar, so I suggest tipping it up once a week to make sure all the fruit is covered. When you open the jar to use the mincemeat, give it a good stir. It will keep for up to 3 months if you can manage to fight off the requests for more.

---

* I use my daughter's old bottle sterilizer to make sure my jars are thoroughly clean. It works with steam and only takes a few minutes.

Mary Wood's Favourite Christmas Recipe – Smoked Salmon and Tuna Mayonnaise Parcels Served on a Crisp Rosti

I'm all for the simple life touched by a little luxury that doesn't cost the earth. My Christmas lunch begins with a starter that I can prepare on Christmas Eve and refrigerate till needed, with very little to do on the day, and it really does fit the remit of simple yet luxurious.

Serves 4

Parcels:

4 slices of smoked salmon, at least 5 cm (2 in.) wide and 15 cm (6 in.) long (you can buy a packet from the deli and cut these yourself, or ask the fishmonger at your local store to do it for you)

1 medium-size tin of tuna in
brine, drained till very dry

Mayonnaise

For the rosti:

2 large fluffy potatoes

2 tablespoons of virgin olive oil

Accompaniments and garnish:

1 lemon cut in 4 wedges

4 sprigs of fresh parsley

Cheats' Melba toast to accompany (cheats'
because I buy a box of ready-made toast)

Butter to serve with toast

*As long as you have room in your fridge you can pre-
pare the parcels on Christmas Eve:*

Mix the tuna and mayonnaise together, trying not
to make the mixture too moist.

Lay out the smoked salmon. Put a heaped des-
sertspoon (or more) of the tuna mixture onto the
end of the smoked salmon and roll. Neaten edges
and refrigerate.

Rostis can also be prepared the evening before:
Peel the potatoes and grate them onto a clean tea

towel. Roll up the tea towel and squeeze to get the potato as dry as possible. Divide into 4 portions and press each one into a rounded shape. Wrap tightly in clingfilm and refrigerate.

Cook and assemble on Christmas morning:
Fry the rostis in the olive oil for 3 to 4 minutes each side until crisp and golden. Leave to one side. Then just before serving reheat in microwave and place each one on a small plate.

The parcels do not need to be cooked. Take from refrigerator just before serving and place one on top of each rosti. Decorate with lemon wedges and parsley, and serve with Melba toast and butter.

extracts reading groups new events

competitions books new events

discounts extracts extracts discounts

competitions extracts reading groups events

books new reading groups discounts

events books extracts events

extracts new titles reading groups

new books interviews new

reading groups events extracts extracts books

books discounts events

extracts new books events interviews new books extracts

events new events

discounts extracts discounts books

www.panmacmillan.com

extracts events reading groups books

competitions books extracts new